You're About to Become a

Privileged Woman.

INTRODUCING
PAGES & PRIVILEGES™.

It's our way of thanking you for buying
our books at your favorite retail store.

—— *GET ALL THIS FREE* ——
WITH JUST ONE PROOF OF PURCHASE:

◆ Hotel Discounts up to 60% at home and abroad

◆ Travel Service - Guaranteed lowest published
   airfares plus 5% cash back on tickets

◆ $25 Travel Voucher

◆ Sensuous Petite Parfumerie collection ($50 value)

◆ Insider Tips Letter with sneak previews of
   upcoming books

◆ Mystery Gift (if you enroll before 6/15/95)

*You'll get a FREE personal card, too.
It's your passport to all these benefits— and to
even more great gifts & benefits to come!*

There's no club to join. No purchase commitment. No obligation.

As a *Privileged Woman,*
you'll be entitled to all
these *Free Benefits.*
And *Free Gifts,* too.

To thank you for buying our books, we've designed an exclusive FREE program called *PAGES & PRIVILEGES*™. You can enroll with just one Proof of Purchase, and get the kind of luxuries that, until now, you could only read about.

*B*IG HOTEL DISCOUNTS

A privileged woman stays in the finest hotels. And so can you—at up to 60% off! Imagine standing in a hotel check-in line and watching as the guest in front of you pays $150 for the same room that's only costing you $60. Your *Pages & Privileges* discounts are good at Sheraton, Marriott, Best Western, Hyatt and thousands of other fine hotels all over the U.S., Canada and Europe.

*F*REE DISCOUNT TRAVEL SERVICE

A privileged woman is always jetting to romantic places. When <u>you</u> fly, just make one phone call for the lowest published airfare at time of booking—<u>or double the difference back</u>! PLUS—

you'll get a $25 voucher to use the first time you book a flight AND <u>5% cash back on every ticket you buy thereafter through the travel service</u>!

*F*REE GIFTS!

A privileged woman is always getting wonderful gifts.
Luxuriate in rich fragrances that will stir your senses (and his). This gift-boxed assortment of fine perfumes includes three popular scents, each in a beautiful designer bottle. <u>Truly Lace</u>...This luxurious fragrance unveils your sensuous side. <u>L'Effleur</u>...discover the romance of the Victorian era with this soft floral. <u>Muguet des bois</u>...a single note floral of singular beauty. This $50 value is yours—FREE when you enroll in *Pages & Privileges* ! And it's just the beginning of the gifts and benefits that will be coming your way!

*F*REE INSIDER TIPS LETTER

A privileged woman is always informed. And you'll be, too, with our free letter full of fascinating information and sneak previews of upcoming books.

*M*ORE GREAT GIFTS & BENEFITS TO COME

A privileged woman always has a lot to look forward to.
And so will you. You get all these wonderful FREE gifts and benefits now with only one purchase...and there are no additional purchases required. However, each additional retail purchase of Harlequin and Silhouette books brings you a step closer to even more great FREE benefits like half-price movie tickets...and even more FREE gifts like these beautiful fragrance gift baskets:

L'Effleur ...This basketful of romance lets you discover L'Effleur from head to toe, heart to home.

Truly Lace ...A basket spun with the sensuous luxuries of Truly Lace, including Dusting Powder in a reusable satin and lace covered box.

*E*NROLL *N*OW!
Complete the Enrollment Form on the back of this card and become a Privileged Woman today!

**Enroll Today in *PAGES & PRIVILEGES*™,
the program that gives you Great Gifts
and Benefits with just one purchase!**

Enrollment Form

☐ *Yes!* I WANT TO BE A *PRIVILEGED WOMAN.*

Enclosed is one *PAGES & PRIVILEGES*™ Proof of Purchase from
any Harlequin or Silhouette book currently for sale in stores (Proofs of
Purchase are found on the back pages of books) and the store cash register
receipt. Please enroll me in *PAGES & PRIVILEGES*™. Send my Welcome
Kit and FREE Gifts -- and activate my FREE benefits -- immediately.

NAME (please print)
_____

ADDRESS _____ APT. NO _____

CITY _____ STATE _____ ZIP/POSTAL CODE _____

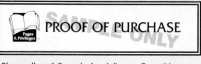
PROOF OF PURCHASE

Please allow 6-8 weeks for delivery. Quantities are
limited. We reserve the right to substitute items.
Enroll before October 31, 1995 and receive
one full year of benefits.

**NO CLUB!
NO COMMITMENT!**
*Just one purchase brings
you great Free Gifts
and Benefits!*
(See inside for details.)

Name of store where this book was purchased_____

Date of purchase_____

Type of store:

☐ Bookstore ☐ Supermarket ☐ Drugstore

☐ Dept. or discount store (e.g. K-Mart or Walmart)

☐ Other (specify)_____

Which Harlequin or Silhouette series do you usually read?

_____

Complete and mail with one Proof of Purchase and store receipt to:

U.S.: *PAGES & PRIVILEGES*™, P.O. Box 1960, Danbury, CT 06813-1960

Canada: *PAGES & PRIVILEGES*™, 49-6A The Donway West, P.O. 813,
North York, ON M3C 2E8   PRINTED IN U.S.A

▶ DETACH HERE AND MAIL TODAY! ▶

"I brought you here because I need a wife,"

Ty said seriously.

"A *wife?*"

"In a word, yes."

Tyler could tell that he'd knocked Emily for a loop. He knew how she felt. This morning, he'd gotten up and gone to work a single, unencumbered, carefree bachelor. This evening, he'd come home with three wacky new family members, who were already turning his apple-pie-order life upside down.

The only hope he had of turning these unlikely crew members into the family of his dreams was the woman seated in front of him. The woman who sat there now, looking at him as if he'd lost his mind.

Dear Reader,

Spring is the perfect time to celebrate the joy of new romance. So get set to fall in love as Silhouette Romance brings you six new wonderful books.

Blaine O'Connor is a *Father in the Making* in Marie Ferrarella's heartwarming FABULOUS FATHERS title. When this handsome bachelor suddenly becomes a full-time dad, he's more than happy to take a few lessons in child rearing from pretty Bridgette Rafanelli. Now he hopes to teach Bridgette a thing or two about love!

Love—Western style—begins this month with a delightful new series, WRANGLERS AND LACE. Each book features irresistible cowboys and the women who tame their wild hearts. The fun begins with *Daddy Was a Cowboy* by Jodi O'Donnell.

In Carolyn Zane's humorous duet, SISTER SWITCH, twin sisters change places and find romance. This time around, sister number two, Emily Brant, meets her match when she pretends sexy Tyler Newroth is her husband in *Weekend Wife*.

Also this month, look for *This Man and This Woman,* an emotional story by Lucy Gordon about a wedding planner who thinks marriage is strictly business—until she meets a dashing Prince Charming of her own. And don't miss *Finally a Family,* Moyra Tarling's tale of a man determined to win back his former love—and be a father to the child he never knew he had. And Margaret Martin makes her debut with *Husband in Waiting.*

Happy Reading!

Anne Canadeo
Senior Editor

Please address questions and book requests to:
Silhouette Reader Service
U.S.: 3010 Walden Ave., P.O. Box 1325, Buffalo, NY 14269
Canadian: P.O. Box 609, Fort Erie, Ont. L2A 5X3

WEEKEND WIFE

Carolyn Zane

Silhouette
ROMANCE™
Published by Silhouette Books
America's Publisher of Contemporary Romance

Dedication:
To the good Lord, with thanks for our home.
Thanks to: My husband, Matt, for his never-ending supply of great ideas.

Acknowledgment:
Thank you, Debbie, for the cruise.

 SILHOUETTE BOOKS

ISBN 0-373-19082-4

WEEKEND WIFE

Printed in U.S.A.

Books by Carolyn Zane

Silhouette Romance

The Wife Next Door #1011
Wife in Name Only #1035
*Unwilling Wife #1063
*Weekend Wife #1082

*Sister Switch

CAROLYN ZANE

lives with her husband, Matt, in the rolling countryside near Portland, Oregon's Willamette River. Their menagerie, which includes two cats, Jazz and Blues, and golden retriever, Bob Barker, was recently joined by baby daughter Madeline. Although Carolyn spent months poring over the baby name books, looking for just the right name for their firstborn, her husband was adamant about calling her Madeline. "After all, Matt plus Carolyn equals Madeline." How could she resist such logic?

So, when Carolyn is not busy changing Maddie, or helping her husband renovate their rambling one-hundred-plus-year-old farmhouse, she makes time to write.

Dear Erica,

Well, sister dear, my experiment posing as a homeless person isn't turning out as I'd expected. I only spent a few days in the role before I met Tyler Newroth and agreed to be his wife.

Now, now, don't go getting too excited. Tyler just needs a temporary wife—for a weekend or two. I'll be going on vacation with him and our daughter (don't ask, it's too complicated). Erica, the man is irresistible! What am I going to do if he should find out who I really am?

Well, I've got to go practice being the perfect wife. I hope everything is fine with Will and the kids.

Love,

Emily

Prologue

Emily Brant adjusted and tightened the thin, dirty blanket to snugly cover the feverish child she cradled in her lap. The night air was so cold. Last week, before she'd begun sleeping outside to study the homeless, she'd thought it was warm all the time in L.A.

Just another one of her many misconceptions, she mused tiredly, and shifted to a more comfortable position. Her arms ached with the weight of the young girl she held. This was so much harder than she'd ever dreamed. She longed to throw in the towel on her thesis project, to go back to Northern California and her comfortable summer job as a nanny, but she couldn't. Not now. Not after spending the last week with Carmen and Helga under this miserable freeway overpass. They needed her.

"How's the kid?" Helga, known in the homeless circles as "the plastic lady," poked her shower-capped head through her garbage bag poncho and looked with concern at the orphan in Emily's arms.

Brushing the dark curls out of the child's face, Emily lightly rested a hand on the warm forehead. "I don't know," she admitted to the eccentric older woman huddled next to her. "It could be a common cold...or it could be worse. She should see a doctor."

Helga swore with the articulation of a seasoned sailor and shook her head. "I just hope it ain't that damn TB. That stuff's a killer," she muttered, and ducked her grizzly old head back down into the dark recesses of her plastic poncho.

Emily's thoughtful frown was determined. It wasn't that bad yet, but if she didn't do something soon, it would be. The eight-year-old girl moaned some nonsensical phrases, half in Spanish, half in English, and again Emily wished that she'd thought to bring at least one credit card with her.

But no, she'd wanted to make her research as authentic as possible. That's what she'd promised the university she would do, and that's what she'd done.

It was authentic, all right, she thought wearily, and settled back against the concrete embankment she now called home. Her stomach growled painfully, reminding her once again that authentic or not, she had to do something to get the three of them some food. And medicine for Carmen.

Raking her dirty hands through her stringy, tangled hair, Emily sighed. But what? What could she do to make money? Where could she go to get help? Briefly she thought about seeking help in one of the local homeless shelters, but they were already far too crowded and she and her two companions would be back out on the street before they knew what hit them. And, according to Helga, Carmen had already been in and out of every orphanage in the county. Emily wanted to weep at the thought. There had to be a better solution.

The thick, never-ending cloud of exhaust rolled off the freeway and Carmen shivered and moaned in her arms. Emily glanced over at the dotty old Helga, surrounded by her mountain of plastic, and knew then and there that if they were ever going to get some help, it was going to be up to her.

Doggedly, Emily shifted Carmen in her arms and reached for her journal—the one possession she'd carried with her to L.A. besides the clothes on her back—and flipped to the day's entry. Pulling her pen out of the notebook's spiral spine, she wrote.

Thursday, July 21. Nearly midnight.
Dear Diary:
As much as I hate to admit it, my enthusiasm for this project is waning. In its place, I'm feeling hopeless and abandoned by society, which, I guess, is a sign that my experiment is working.

This week I have seen so much sickness, crime and despair, I wonder what possible difference my little thesis project could make. I have learned, however, that even in the sorriest of situations, there is beauty.

Carmen is so delightful, despite the circumstances. Childlike and playful, and remarkably well-adjusted, considering the tragedy she has endured in her short life. And, Helga, though she is as rough around the edges as a saw blade, has a tender heart... although I suspect she may not be in the best of health, her racking cough sometimes frightens me.

Today, Carmen was feverish and completely listless. I have to get them both some good food and medicine soon. Or I fear what may become of them.

I guess I'll do what I have to do to get work or money. I'll exhaust every avenue available to me without ID or help from friends and colleagues, and then, if I'm unsuccessful, I'll call my sister Erica and ask her to wire me some money. But only as a last resort. I still intend to maintain the integrity of this project....

Helga hacked and wheezed from the bowels of her plastic dome as Emily finished her latest entry. Yes, she re-

solved, and firmly closed her journal. Tomorrow, come hell
or high water—which was a distinct possibility, given the
fact that they were in L.A.—she would find a way to pro-
vide food and shelter for these two wayfaring souls she'd
come to love so much.

Chapter One

Tyler Newroth tugged at the tie that threatened to strangle him. This meeting was not going at all the way he'd expected. It had to be some kind of joke. Had anyone told him before his transfer that his new, power-driven boss would likely be attracted to him, he'd have been flattered. But, had they told him her attraction could prove fatal—to his promising career—he'd have turned down this lucrative promotion in a hot New York second. Let some other poor fool be her boy toy. He had work to do.

Roxanne Delmonico leaned over Ty's desk and looked him straight in the eye. Her considerable endowments preceded her as she tapped her perfectly lacquered nails on his desktop. "Well?" she purred. "How do you like your new job? The West Coast division of Connstarr is run somewhat . . . differently than the East Coast."

That much had been obvious to Ty his first ten minutes on the job. From the second he'd walked into his new office three days ago, he had been literally chased around his desk by one Roxanne Delmonico, Vice President, West

Coast Division, Connstarr Enterprises, and niece to Denny Delmonico, owner of the company. In all his years at Connstarr, this had never happened to him before. The East Coast division in Boston was run by a bunch of stuffy, old, cigar-smoking men. None of them had ever played stupid mind games with him. Or come on to him.

Yes, Tyler decided, his nerves wound tighter than the rubber bands inside a golf ball, there was some serious sexual harassment going on here, and it wasn't coming from him.

"Well…" Ty cleared his throat. "I will admit there seems to be a little, uh, looser atmosphere out here."

Roxanne's bridgework sparkled as she threw back her head and laughed throatily. "Oh, Ty, baby. Really. You're going to have to loosen up if you want to fit in around here. Come on! You're so uptight!" Her smile was beguiling as her lips parted to reveal a set of perfectly capped teeth. In a single, feline movement, she hiked a very curvaceous hip up onto his desk.

Was this bimbo kidding? Tyler fought the urge to laugh out loud. She was something straight out of a bad B-grade movie. This whole situation would have been uproariously funny if he didn't have the unnerving feeling that she was serious. He could read a veiled threat a mile away. *Come across, Ty, baby, or else.* That's what she really meant.

Loosen up. Yeah, right, sure. Just the shot in the arm his career needed. A toss in the hay with Jezebel here, and he'd be out on his ear in no time. No thanks. His career was far too important for him to jeopardize by putting it into Roxanne's sleazy clutches. Ty preferred to make it to the top because of his sterling reputation as a businessman. Not by conquering a basket case like Roxanne.

Ignoring his stony silence, Roxanne pouted prettily, pursing her moist red lips as though posing for a soap opera close-up. "You know, I've been thinking…" She sighed, her voice husky with meaning. "Since you and I are going to be working so closely together, we should probably make an effort to get to know each other a lot better. Say, over dinner? Perhaps this weekend?" She gazed at him, her hawk-like eyes missing nothing.

Oh, for crying out loud. Why hadn't he anticipated this question? "Well, uh..." Tyler's mind was pitching and rolling, frantically searching for a way out of this politically sticky situation. Being new to his position as director of national accounts for Connstarr, one of the nation's leading software companies, he had no desire to rock the boat his third day on the job.

But by the same token, if and when he ever decided to spend the weekend with a nymphomaniac, it would be one of his own choosing. Not one who could fire him if she didn't like his performance. How the hell had he gotten into this mess? He didn't want to have to resort to drastic measures to deal with this situation, but if she kept pushing, he didn't know what else he could do. "Can I let you know?"

Roxanne laughed. "Sure, silly. But you don't have much time. It's Friday."

Thank God for that much, Ty thought as he watched her swing her shapely stocking-clad legs up onto his desk—which was no simple task considering the snugness of her skirt. He leaned back in his chair as she strained across his desk, arching her back and tossing her big, blond hair over her shoulders.

In coy sotto voce, she suggested, "We could try out my little Welcome to L.A. gift, if you're game."

"Welcome to L.A.?"

"Didn't you find it? I put it in your filing cabinet," she whispered conspiratorially.

Tyler ran a hand over the muscle that jumped in his jaw. "That was *you?*" He choked and tried to keep the shock out of his voice. He hadn't dreamed that even Roxanne could be that tacky. He'd assumed that the bottle of champagne wrapped in sexy female lingerie and tied so fetchingly with handcuffs had been a practical joke sent by his buddies at Connstarr's Boston division.

"So," she pressed, relentless in her pursuit. "What do you say? You. Me. Tomorrow night? I can promise you'll have an excellent time."

Ty's heart slammed against his ribs with a sickening thud. What on earth was he going to do with this nut case? The nut case who now held the key to his future at Connstarr.

He had to take control of this situation, he resolved, trying to tie the pencil he held into a frustrated knot. And he had to do it now, before it got further out of hand. The time to take a drastic measure was now. But how? How could he fend off her advances without provoking her ire?

Before he knew what came over him, he heard himself blurt out, "Under any other circumstances, Roxanne, I'm sure you're right. Getting a little better acquainted for professional purposes would be a nice idea." His smile was professional and aloof as he deliberately misunderstood her double meaning. "However, I promised my wife I'd spend some time with her this weekend." *This was brilliant!* Why hadn't he thought of it before? Surely she'd leave him alone if she thought he was married. Mentally congratulating himself on his stroke of genius, he sat back and waited for her to bow out gracefully.

Roxanne's heavily made-up eyes narrowed suspiciously. "I was under the distinct impression that you were not married." Her smile was hard.

Uh-oh. She wasn't taking this quite the way he'd hoped. The ruthless look in her eyes made him sick. Big deal. He'd thrown down the gauntlet and he would see this battle through to the end.

"You were?" Tyler tugged at the knot in his tie. He suddenly needed air. Then again, maybe lying wasn't such a good idea, after all.

"Your file says you're single." She arched an inquisitive eyebrow at him.

"Hmm…yes," he hedged, crossing his fingers behind his back. "Well, it just happened a short while ago, actually." He was getting in deep here. But what else could he do, short of accusing his brand-new boss—the owner's niece, no less—of harassing him sexually. Not the impression he wanted to make, his first week on the job.

Sliding one high-heeled foot up alongside her knee, she looked over her shoulder at Ty through narrow, suspicious eyes. "Tell me about her," she demanded.

Groaning inwardly, Ty dipped his brush and continued to paint his way toward the corner of doom. "She's a lovely woman. We were...u-uh..." he stammered, trying to organize his jumbled thoughts into some sort of plausible explanation. "High school sweethearts."

"But you only *just now* decided to...tie the knot?"

The pencil Ty was holding snapped in two. "Just now," he echoed brightly. "I just couldn't stand to leave her in Boston."

Roxanne smirked. "Isn't that sweet?" she drawled, and buffed a bloodred nail on her designer silk blouse.

Fidgeting in his leather chair, Ty nodded noncommittally. "You'd love her," he predicted, hoping the likelihood of Roxanne ever wanting to actually meet his wife was slim to none.

"I'm sure." Roxanne was clearly not buying his trumped-up story. "Well, I must meet her sometime soon, and really get to know her." She stretched languidly. "After all, we will be spending the entire week together soon."

Puzzled, Tyler asked, "We will?"

Roxanne threw back her head of wild hair and laughed huskily. "Have you forgotten the company cruise? We sail next week." Her piercing look sent a chill up Tyler's spine.

Damn. He had forgotten about the cruise Connstarr was treating its management team and their families to next week. With the headaches of transferring to L.A. from Boston, and then the disgusting reality of Roxanne as a boss, it had completely slipped his mind.

His heart slid from his throat to the pit of his stomach and landed with a defeated plop. Where the heck was he going to get a wife at this late date?

Smiling a tiny smile, Roxanne said, "I expect you'll be bringing her? I hear everyone will be bringing their families . . . *if* they have them."

"Oh, yes." Tyler was sweating profusely now. "She's been looking forward to it."

"How cute." Her tone dripped with sarcasm. "I must admit I am disappointed." She sighed. "I thought you would be going by yourself. But I imagine we'll find a way to have some fun, anyway," she said suggestively.

Ty shook his head imperceptibly, still unable to believe her incredible audacity.

Roxanne's expression grew suddenly bitter as she swung her legs over the edge of his desk and levered herself up to stand next to him. "I was married once," she admitted in a moment of true candor.

"Oh?" What happened? Had she killed and eaten him? Ty wondered absently as he waited for his new boss to continue.

"Yes. I found marriage too . . . confining."

He was surprised at the depth of emotion that flashed briefly across her carefully painted facade. "Confining?"

"Yes." The look was suddenly gone, replaced instead with her usual sultry expression. "You will, too, a man like you. Mark my words."

"Like me?"

"Uh-huh," she purred. "You must know how irresistible you are." Appraising him boldly with appreciative eyes, Roxanne continued. "All that thick, dark, gorgeous hair, those sexy, green, bedroom eyes—" she winked at him "—that . . . mmm, hard body. Not to mention your incredible talent here at Connstarr." Abruptly she extended a businesslike hand. "It will be a *pleasure* working with you, I'm sure."

Not about to return her loaded compliment, Tyler briefly shook her hand. "Thanks." His reply was curt as he escorted her to his office door.

Roxanne paused in the doorway and adjusted the handkerchief in Ty's jacket pocket. "I'm looking forward to meeting your . . . wife. We must get together soon." Laughing as though skeptical at his sudden change in marital status, she patted him on the cheek and disappeared down the hall.

For crimeny sakes, now he had just over a week to find a suitable wife. It wasn't as if he didn't have enough on his plate already with his new job and living in a new city, he didn't even know anyone well enough to date, let alone marry. He ran a tired hand over his jaw. In the next few days maybe he could find an out-of-work actress who could do the job. Hollywood must be crawling with them. Surely he could find someone by then.

Emily wiped the perspiration from her brow with a soiled handkerchief and sighed. She was obviously not cut out to be a beggar. Holding her crude cardboard sign up a little higher to shield herself from the sun's blistering rays, she turned to check on Carmen and Helga.

Seated on a grassy freeway divider, they huddled together in the shade of an exit sign and waited for the words on Emily's torn cardboard to work their magic. Will Work For Food. Emily had assured them that morning that this was their ticket to a filling meal and maybe even a decent place to sleep. Now, after a grueling morning in the hot L.A. sun, she wasn't so sure.

So far, the only thing she *was* sure of was that she had encountered every kind of crackpot that Interstate 5 had to offer. The weirdos were out in force, and Emily had met and rejected them all.

At first Emily had hoped her benefactor would be a kindly old man or woman. At least that way she'd feel safe. But that morning when a pistol-packin' granny had pulled up and claimed she needed some assistance with her target practice, Emily had thanked her for her gracious offer and sent her on her way.

"You're sure now, dear?" she had inquired sweetly just before pulling away. "It's easy work, really. You just have to stand very still."

Then she'd longed for a nice young couple. Perhaps someone who needed a lawn mowed or a car washed. What she got was an invitation to join Mr. and Mrs. Party for some questionable social activities after-hours that night.

"Yes," Mr. Party had confided in a low voice. "You are just what we're looking for. Someone with connections. Someone who could score us some party favors, heh-heh, if you know what I mean."

Emily hadn't known, and hadn't wanted to know.

Maybe a nice family would be more her style, she'd decided, until one self-righteous family man had thrown his hamburger at her and suggested that she "get her sorry butt off the freeway."

Her feelings were hurt, her feet ached, and she was beginning to believe that there wasn't a single soul on this godforsaken freeway that cared if she lived or died.

"Hey, lady! Wanna party?"

The voices of six, grungy-looking teenage boys in a convertible snapped her out of her depressing reverie. Howling and catcalling, they pulled onto the shoulder and shouted obscenities at her.

Emily nervously nibbled her lip. "No," she called over the lump of fear that lodged so tightly in her throat she could barely breathe. Knuckles white, she shakily gripped her sign in front of her face as a flimsy barrier against their leering, wolfish expressions.

"Too bad. Your loss!" they jeered as, tires spinning in the gravel, they disappeared into the sea of warped and heartless people that made up this uncaring world.

Sighing with extreme relief, Emily dropped her sign on the freeway shoulder and walked on rubber legs over to join Helga and Carmen in the shade.

"Time for a break," she announced in a shallow, shaky voice, doing her best to sound optimistic.

Helga muttered a few juicy expletives under her breath. "Bunch of damn creeps out there," she shouted at the noisy freeway, and shook an empty plastic milk container at a passing truck for good measure. "And those people out there have the nerve to think I'm weird." Again she swore colorfully.

For the first time that morning Emily's smile was real. How she loved Helga's feisty spirit. "How are you two doing?" she asked, and chucked Carmen playfully under her soft, smooth chin.

"We're doin' okay. I could use a smoke and a drink, and the same for my friend Carmen here," Helga said dryly, causing the child to giggle. "Yeah. And a massage. That would be nice."

"I'll see what I can do." Emily grinned. Turning to Carmen, she stroked the girl's midnight black hair and looked into her large, clear brown eyes. "You look like you might be feeling a little better, *sí?*"

"*Sí.*" Carmen nodded and sneezed.

Emily frowned. "If someone doesn't stop and give us some help by the end of the day, we'll need to start thinking about what to do next, okay?"

Shrugging, Carmen smiled widely.

Helga snorted. "Ain't nobody gonna stop and help us, so you may as well give up and let me teach you how to strip. I know a place you could work where the tips are great." She paused, her brow furrowed thoughtfully. "At least, they used to be."

"Thanks, Helga. I'll keep that in mind. In the meantime, I'd better get back to work. You never know when our knight in shining armor could pull up."

Helga let loose with a string of skeptical expletives and, rolling her eyes, disappeared into her multilayered plastic ensemble.

Doggedly, Emily rose and strode to the edge of the freeway where she picked up her cardboard plea for help. What she wouldn't give for a filling meal and a hot shower. And sheets. Clean, crispy, linen sheets would sure feel good against freshly shaved legs.

Someone out there just had to care. Someone normal and nice, who would offer her a legitimate job. Someone who could make a difference in the lives of these two homeless people. Yes, she thought determinedly. She would know them when she saw them. Until then, she would just have faith and wait.

Rush hour. The perfect capper to a world-class lousy day. Tyler slowly inched forward on the interstate and tried to think calming thoughts. But it was useless. Grinding his teeth in frustration, he shoved his new Mercedes into low, and resigned himself to the fact that it would be at least another hour before he arrived home. Until then he was stuck on this rotten freeway with nothing to do but nurse his fledgling ulcer.

What on earth had possessed him to lie to Roxanne? he wondered, groaning out loud at his stupidity. Why hadn't he just told her what she could do with her crummy job? Exhaling noisily, he knew the answer. Because he had worked too damn long and too damn hard to let the owner's bimbo niece get in the way of his fast-track career. He knew from experience that people like Roxanne eventually got what they deserved. The trick was hanging in there until they hung themselves. And Tyler was determined to hang in there till the bitter end. If only for the satisfaction of watching Roxanne's demise.

As he flexed his hands on the steering wheel, wishing it were Roxanne's heavily perfumed neck, his car phone rang.

"Newroth," he barked into the mouthpiece. He was in no mood for a conversation.

"Well, well, well," came the husky voice. "Is that any way to talk to the boss?" Roxanne giggled girlishly.

Damn it! Now he couldn't even escape this viper in the privacy of his own traffic jam. Modern science had definitely gone too far.

"Hello, Roxanne." Tyler schooled his voice to not give away his exceeding frustration. "What can I do for you?"

Roxanne laughed suggestively. "I've been giving that some thought."

His single-handed grip tightened on the steering wheel.

"Actually, it's not what you can do for me. It's Uncle Denny. He and I will be entertaining a personal friend and potentially very lucrative client this Monday night. He wants you to be at the meeting."

"Sure," Tyler said. "Where will we meet?"

"Uncle Denny has a bunch of season passes to the Dodger games. Box seats."

"Sounds great. Count me in."

"Good," Roxanne purred. "Oh, and, Tyler? Uncle Denny wants to meet your wife. He sends his heartiest congratulations on your recent...*nuptials* and requests that you bring her to the game. The client has a thing about family men, so your timing is perfect." Roxanne's irreverent laugh tinkled delightedly across the line.

"That will be fine." He choked. Tyler sat in shock as Roxanne obviously relished his discomfort. So she thought she was on to his little ruse. Well, damn it all, she was. But he couldn't let her know that. Not yet. "We'd love to attend," he said, trying to sound as self-confident as possible.

"You would?" Roxanne seemed surprised.

"Absolutely," Tyler lied. *Oh, holy cow, great day in the morning! He was up the creek without a paddle now.*

"Super. See you there," she breathed, and hung up.

"See you there." Ty echoed, and wished someone would just drive by and shoot him. He was in the heart of the city for Pete's sake, where was a weapon-toting gangster when you needed one?

And just where the hell was he going to get a wife over the weekend? Letting out a primal scream, he beat the dashboard in frustration. That witch would be the death of him yet.

Thinking back on his fruitless calls to the Hollywood talent agencies that afternoon, Ty downed half a pack of antacids as a bad case of heartburn smoldered in his churning gut. He had called too late. No one, it seemed, could rush to his aid this weekend and begin rehearsals for a week-long cruise as Mrs. Tyler Newroth. Friday afternoons were a bad time to call, he'd been informed.

He had considered running an ad in the Personals section of the *Times*. But by the time the ad made it to the paper, and he had screened and interviewed the applicants, and eventually hired Mrs. Right, the cruise ship would have sailed without him.

Feeling desperate, Tyler suddenly realized that he now had less than forty-eight hours to come up with a wife. For once in his life, he dearly wished he were married. It had never seemed that important before now. He'd been happily married to his career for years, and his casual dating life kept him entertained. Besides, he was only twenty-nine years old. He had aeons of time to settle down.

"Wrong-o, you big jerk," he chastised himself out loud. *You have forty-eight hours.*

There just had to be a wonderful, warm, caring, reasonably attractive woman out there who could play the part. Someone who needed work. Someone who wouldn't mind picking up and leaving at the drop of a hat. Someone...as desperate as he was.

"Fat chance." He sighed, and slowly rolled a few inches farther down the freeway. Yep, he was definitely dead meat.

Uh-oh. She was dead meat now. Emily felt her mouth dry up like the Mojave desert as what absolutely had to be a pimp pulled off onto the shoulder in his bright pink, vintage Cadillac. After slowly unfurling his lanky body from the seamy interior of his gaudy car, he closed the door with a flourish and sauntered jauntily in her direction.

Emily tightly gripped her cardboard sign for support and glanced back at Helga and Carmen. *Oh, no!* Her knees shook violently at his approach and, as a wave of nausea washed over her, she was sure she was going to faint dead away. She wasn't ready to be a filly in some sleazoid pervert's idea of a stable. His gold tooth gleamed evilly in the afternoon sunlight as he sauntered down the shoulder toward her, wearing a wolfish smile. Emily smiled as bravely as she could in return and began to back up toward Helga and Carmen.

Frantically her mind searched for an escape route, for herself and her two innocent companions. Carmen and Helga weren't up to running for their lives, she was sure. And she'd be damned if she'd ever allow either of them to become love slaves to this...this...miscreant dirtbag. She stopped walking and thought about what she was doing. She was leading the wolf to the sheep, that's what she was doing. Uh-oh. No, better take this particular dirtbag by the horns and get rid of him herself.

With a confidence she was nowhere near feeling, she stood her ground until he approached, and was shocked by how truly nasty he looked up close.

"Hello, there," she chirped, in her best Little Mary Sunshine voice. "What can I do for you?"

"Well, I was just noticin' yer sign there, little gal," he mumbled around the toothpick in his mouth.

Her sign was the last thing he was noticing, if his roving eyes were any indication. Emily fidgeted uncomfortably. "Oh, that." *Darn it, anyway.* She was sick and tired of having these ridiculous job interviews with potential employers who should probably be behind bars. "I was just using that to shade myself from the sun," she explained somewhat lamely.

"Says you'll work for food." The dirtbag spat on the ground and pointed at her sign with his frayed toothpick.

She'd play dumb. "It does? Imagine that."

The dirtbag rolled his eyes. "Come on, honey. You need work. I gotta job. It's that simple. Just come with me and I'll fix ya up real good."

"Oh, no. I'm fine. Really. Thank you, though," she hedged, and started to back slowly away.

Not easily dissuaded, the dirtbag followed her. "Oh, come on now, sweetheart," he cajoled, his tone dripping with honey. "You could make some serious money workin' for me. Why a little gal with your looks and figure could go far."

Now Emily knew he was deranged. What looks? She had the looks of a desperate, filthy vagabond. Nervously she pushed at her grimy hair with sweaty palms, and tried to slow her hammering heart. How the hell had she gotten herself into this mess?

Her twin sister had tried to warn her. Told her she was crazy to risk her life living among the homeless for her thesis project. But would she listen? No. And now...well, now Erica would finally realize her dream of being an only child. Her yen to help the down-and-out had always driven Erica crazy, she thought frantically as her life flashed before her eyes.

Standing here, watching the dirtbag eyeball her, she could finally admit that her sister was right. She was nuts. Always had been.

All her life she was the twin that took up the cause of the underdog, took in the stray, couldn't resist the person in trouble, no matter how deep. She and Erica may look exactly alike, but they couldn't be any more different.

Erica had inherited all of the sensible, levelheaded genes, and she had gotten the bleeding heart. And to think that she'd fast-talked her poor, uptight sister into pretending to be her this summer in her regular summer job as the Spencer family's nanny... for this! To be killed by a dirtbag on the interstate in L.A.

Tears of self-pity welled in her eyes. And dang it anyway, she'd left all her ID at home in San Francisco. No one would even know who she was after this guy killed her. What an idiot. Make that, ultra-idiot, she thought, and wondered how one fashioned a deadly weapon out of a piece of cardboard.

What an idiotic thing to do. After slowly coasting mile after endless mile toward home, Tyler had come to the conclusion that he had made a huge mistake in telling Roxanne that he was married. He was in deep, deep trouble and, short of a miracle, he didn't see any way out.

Now the owner of the company and the client of the century were mixed up in this ridiculous charade, and Monday night he would have to let them down. Unless...

Tyler's mind was momentarily taken off his troubles as he slowly cruised by what looked like a young beggar woman clutching a sign that read Will Work For Food. Some motley character was standing next to her, obviously trying to hire her services.

She looked desperate. He knew the feeling. She needed a job. He needed a woman. They needed each other.

Back off, buddy, he thought fiercely as he suddenly found himself veering off the freeway and getting out of his car. *She's mine.*

Was he crazy? The closer he got, the more he could see she looked like something out of a Charles Dickens novel. He tried to envision himself introducing her to Connstarr's owner. *Sir, I'd like you to meet my wife, Olive Twist....*

And Roxanne. He was sure she'd die laughing.

What the hell. At this point he didn't give a rat's rear end. She was better than nothing. And who could tell, maybe she'd clean up nicely.

Although Tyler had little experience with the plight of the homeless, his heart melted at the sight of this plucky little thing standing her ground against the loser with the gold tooth. His dislike for this guy was instant and profound.

"Hey!" Ty called, smiling broadly at the little vagabond whose eyes were filled with terror. "I saw your sign and wondered if, uh, you weren't already taken—" he nodded politely at the loser "—if I could offer you a job."

"No!" she cried hastily, and then, looking confused at her reply, amended, "I mean, no, I'm not already taken."

"Great. Why don't you come with me now and you can get started?" Ty watched her look back and forth between the two men, as though trying to figure out which was the lesser of two evils. Her hands shook as they gripped her tattered piece of cardboard. He had to admire her caution, after all, he was a stranger, too.

"What kind of work?" she asked suspiciously as she looked him over from head to toe.

"Oh, uh, well, it's a long story, actually." He fumbled for words that wouldn't scare her off. She was probably his last chance, and he didn't want to frighten her away by seeming too desperate. "But it's a good job, with good pay, and I can offer you a room and meals." Noting how her eyes kept darting fearfully to the gold-toothed loser, he added, "Nothing you don't want to do." He shot a meaningful glance in the loser's direction.

The loser grew impatient. "Hey, now! I think I was here before y'all." His eyes narrowed at Ty.

"So you were," Ty admitted genially. "I guess we'll have to go with what the lady wants." *Please want me, please want me,* he silently pleaded in his head. Yes, he admitted forlornly to himself, Roxanne had reduced him to a pathetic, groveling wreck.

"No!" The loser was through fooling around. "She goes with me. I found her, she's mine."

At this point the little waif, quaking in her boots, moved behind Ty for protection. She seemed so frail and helpless, Ty felt a sudden urge to protect her against this scumbag.

"I'm afraid not, buddy," he said, drawing himself up to his full six-foot-two height. "She not some piece of meat that you can claim just because you saw her first."

The loser's eyes narrowed. "Says who?"

"Says me," Ty said fiercely, and took a threatening step toward him. He didn't want to get into some kind of barroom brawl with this idiot right here on the edge of the freeway, but if that's what it took, let the party begin. He figured he didn't have anything to lose.

"Who the hell are you?"

Ty rolled his eyes. For crying out loud, what difference did that make? "I'm your worst nightmare," he bluffed, borrowing some line out of an action movie. "So, go ahead. Make my day." He flexed his fists threateningly and glanced behind him at the little waif. She was laughing. Some gratitude, he fumed, and turned back to the loser.

"If you don't have any further business to conduct here, feel free to take off," Ty encouraged, his jaw set with grim determination.

Put out that he'd wasted part of a precious afternoon on this lost cause, the loser went ballistic with a string of hair-singeing curses. When he'd finished telling them both where they could go and what they could do when they got there, he finally spun on his heel and stalked off toward his waiting car.

Tyler heard an audible sigh of relief come from over his shoulder. He turned around to find her right behind him, pale and shaking like a leaf.

"Thank you so much," the waif said, her eyes filled with gratitude. "I was really starting to worry there. I, uh—" she blushed furiously and ran a light hand over her unwashed hair in a singularly feminine gesture "—guess I'm not very good at this business yet. . . ." She let her sentence trail off and her eyes darted humbly to her sign.

Her words and voice had a cultured sound that took Tyler by surprise. He wasn't sure what he'd expected, but this sure as heck wasn't it. "Anytime," he said, and nodded pleasantly at her. "What's your name?" He tried not to let his excitement show.

"Emily," came her sweet reply.

Emily. What a beautiful name. It fit her somehow. "Nice to meet you, Emily. I'm Tyler Newroth." He extended his hand and enveloped her soft, delicate hand in his. Amazing. He'd expected them to be rough and callused from years of hard living. But instead they were as smooth and fragile as rose petals. "Actually, Emily, if you don't have any better offers, I do have a little job for you. It would only take a weekend—or two—of your time, and I swear the pay would be great." At this point, he was ready to split his inheritance with her.

She regarded him warily. "Just what would I have to do for this excellent pay?" she asked, raising a skeptical eyebrow.

Guessing the direction of her thoughts, he shook his head emphatically. "Nothing like that jerk had in mind, if that's what you're asking. This is strictly on the up-and-up." He paused, and corrected himself. "Well, it's legal, anyway."

She smiled doubtfully up at him. "If you say so. There's just one small thing." She glanced over her shoulder at her two traveling companions. "They come with me as part of the deal." Her voice brooked no argument.

"Fine." He was in no mood to quibble. The more the merrier.

The old bird could play the mother-in-law, and the kid... well, the kid could be the kid. It was perfect. Giving himself a mental pat on the back, he followed Emily to where they sat waiting. Hot damn. He was going on a cruise with his loving wife and family. Eat your heart out, Roxanne, he nearly crowed out loud.

He felt a twinge of doubt as he neared the kooky old woman and her shopping cart full of plastic goods. Oh, well, he rationalized as he glanced over his shoulder at his showroom-condition Mercedes, they still had a week to rehearse.

Chapter Two

"Uh, I hate to be a spoilsport..." Ty kept his voice low so that only Emily could hear. "But do we have to bring *that?*" He pointed to the odd assortment of plastic goods that Helga had stored in the broken-down grocery cart.

Emily looked up at him in surprise. "Of course," she said matter-of-factly. "That little cart holds all of her worldly possessions."

"But..." Ty cringed at the thought of stuffing that smelly, dirty, drippy mess into his pristine trunk. "I have a bunch of plastic bags and containers at my house. New ones. I'll be glad to give her all she wants."

Lifting her slender shoulders lightly, Emily shook her head. "It's not the same thing at all."

Of course not, Ty thought sourly. He'd only had a mother-in-law for ten minutes and already she was driving him nuts.

"Well, let's get this show on the road," he muttered, and shrugged out of his jacket in preparation to muscle the old biddy's garbage heap into his trunk. *Yes. He would get Roxanne for this someday.*

Helga hustled forward and directed his every move with the grace and vocabulary of a seasoned fishwife. "Careful with my stuff there, you meathead," she roared when a wheel from her cart caught on his trunk lid and some of its contents spilled to the ground. "Don't screw with my stuff!" she shouted when he nearly lost his grip on the entire mess.

"I wouldn't dream of it," he grunted, staggering under the load. Unfortunately, it was impossible for him to hold his breath against the stench of her "stuff" and load it into the car at the same time. Ty was beginning to think that maybe he'd made his second big mistake of the day. Would he ever be able to make silk purses out of these sows' ears? He'd had a hard childhood, practically a street urchin himself, but he'd clawed his way to the top because he'd had brains and ambition. Did these have-nots have what it took?

It didn't matter. Nothing mattered but getting Roxanne off his case. He was just desperate enough to delude himself into thinking that this would work. Finally completing the odious task, Ty dusted off his hands and turned to Emily. "Okay." He looked around. "Where's your stuff?"

Emily grinned up at him, and Ty was taken aback by the beauty of her smile. Even through the streaks of dirt and grime, something about this woman screamed class. Funny how this destitute woman had more class in her little finger than Roxanne had in her whole body.

Holding up a spiral notebook in one hand, and the dark-haired child's hand in the other, she said, "This is my stuff."

"That's all?" Ty was incredulous. How could someone survive with nothing but a notebook? And what on earth could she possibly need that for?

"Yes," she replied simply. "We're ready to go if you are."

Again she smiled at him, smoothed back her hair, and straightened her collar with a quick, self-conscious gesture. And again Ty was surprised by the gentle elegance she exuded in spite of her unfortunate circumstances. He was dying to know how she came to be homeless.

Smiling down at her, he said, "I'm ready."

"Dadburnit!" Helga thundered from behind him. "Then stop staring and get your skinny butt in the car. We ain't got all damn night here. I still gotta set up camp when we get to your place. Move it," she ordered and, throwing the driver's seat forward, squeezed her generous rump into the back seat of Ty's Mercedes.

Emily smothered a giggle behind her hand and looked up at Ty's stunned face through her heavily fringed eyelashes.

"Your mother takes a little getting used to." He gulped and nodded in Helga's direction. *And he had to convince Roxanne that he'd married into this family?*

Emily led Carmen to the car. "Oh, she's not my mother," she tossed over her shoulder as she helped the child into the back seat and carefully fastened her seat belt. When she was finished, she stood and looked at Ty over the shiny roof of his car.

"She's not?" For some reason, he was incredibly relieved.

"No," she said, and didn't elaborate. "We'd better get her home. She has a lot to do before dark."

With those words to add fuel to his indigestion, Tyler got into the car and pulled onto the interstate, the old woman's plastic goods swirling out of his trunk behind them.

Though they had probably only been driving for a few minutes, it seemed like forever to Emily. Why on earth was it taking so long to get to his house? Hadn't he said that he lived close by?

Glancing over at the tense expression on this handsome stranger's face, Emily grew suddenly worried. Just what did she know about this guy, anyway? What if he was some kind of serial killer? Her eyes darted nervously to the speedometer, and she wondered how she could get Helga and Carmen safely out of the back seat of his car at fifty miles per hour.

Carmen sneezed several times from the seat behind her, and Emily, resigning herself to her fate, decided to take her chances with this stranger. After all, this is what being homeless was all about, wasn't it? Living on the edge? If she wanted her thesis to be authentic, she had to take some chances.

Once again, she slid a sidelong glance over at the polished professional behind the wheel, and wondered what a good-looking guy like him would want from a street person like herself. She knew he hadn't given her all the details about her new job, and it was obvious that he was hiding something. Maybe he was some kind of pervert.

Was it his habit to kidnap young women into kinky love slavery? She shivered with fear until she remembered what she looked like, and then nearly laughed out loud. Some love slave she'd make. She hadn't seen a bottle of shampoo in well over a week, and her carefully manicured nails had broken off days ago. Chewing on her lip, she wished she at least had a tube of lipstick. Then she rolled her eyes, wondering how much better her grubby face would look with a coat of dewy lilac frost on her lips.

What the heck was she thinking, anyway? She didn't care if this sexy stranger thought she was pretty or not. No. She was here for one purpose and one purpose only. To get help for Carmen and Helga, and hopefully to gather some research for her project along the way.

He must have felt the intensity of her stare, because Tyler Newroth slowly turned to look at Emily and favored her with one of the sexiest, most genuine, heart-melting smiles that she'd ever seen. And suddenly, for reasons she couldn't fathom at the moment, Emily knew that they were safe.

She didn't know how she knew, exactly, but she knew. The same way she felt that this man had desperately needed her help back there at the side of the road. Even after a nightmarish week on the streets of L.A., she was still a sucker for anyone in trouble. But just what kind of trouble was this guy in?

"It won't be long now." He kept his voice low, so as not to disturb Helga, who was snoring like a log truck in the back. "We should be there in about ten minutes or so."

"Your house?"

"Yes." He grinned sheepishly at her. "It's kind of a mess, actually. I just moved here from Boston, and I still have a lot of unpacking to do."

Why he should bother explaining to her that his house was a mess, Emily would never know. A bombed-out room at the Beirut Hotel was preferable to where they'd been sleeping. "Is that why you need my help? To get you settled here in L.A.?" She hoped so. Unpacking was a task she could handle.

"In a way, yes," Tyler hedged. "I'll fill you in on all the details as soon as we get home. It really is kind of a long story."

Much to her mortification, Emily's stomach chose that moment to growl in cranky protest of its neglect.

"How does pizza sound?" Ty asked.

Once more Emily's stomach rumbled rudely. "Heavenly." She sighed.

Picking up his car phone, he hit one of the speed dial buttons and grinned at her. "This is how us bachelors cook."

Funny how it was so easy for him to take life's little conveniences for granted. Having spent the last week eating from the occasional can of beans she was able to scrounge up and share with Helga and Carmen, a pizza, ordered from a car phone, made Emily want to weep with joy.

"What do you like?"

"Everything," she breathed.

He glanced back at Helga. "Probably better get a couple of them, huh?"

Emily nodded happily. "At least." She knew she could eat one all by herself.

* * *

Shortly after placing his pizza order, Tyler nosed his Mercedes through the gates of the Rolling Heights Estates. Emily's eyes widened in surprise as he cruised past dozens of opulent mini-mansions nestled into the hills overlooking the magnificent Pacific Ocean.

Looking down at her filthy jeans and shoes, Emily suddenly felt like one of the Beverly Hillbillies after the kinfolk said, "Californy is the place you oughta be." She began to hum under her breath as the stunning residences of California's elite rolled by. *So they loaded up the Mercedes and they moved to—* Wow!

Tyler pushed a button that was clipped to his sun visor and two large iron gates, attached to an impressive brick-and-ironwork fence, swung open to allow them to pass. As he drove down the cobblestone drive and slipped into the portico, the gates slid silently shut behind them.

Manicured box hedges lined the driveway and divided smaller areas off for rose gardens and fountains. The rambling Spanish-style house was crawling with ivy and, as far as Emily could tell, seemed to go on forever. From where she sat under the portico, she could see the kidney-shaped pool, cabana, and a large, landscaped patio area that must make for wonderful parties.

Emily was beginning to wonder if she'd been hit by a car on the freeway. She was sure she'd died and that St. Peter was lurking somewhere beyond that fabulous pool. Sighing, she smiled up at Tyler.

"The pizza should be here in about half an hour or so," Ty said as he pulled his keys out of the ignition. "That should give us enough time to get you settled in." An earthshaking snore came from the back seat. "I hope." He looked doubtful.

"Sure." She nodded encouragingly at him. "Why don't you get Helga's cart out of your trunk, and I'll get these guys up?"

"Sounds like a plan." Ty nodded, unfastening his seat belt. He disappeared toward the back of the car to wrestle with Helga's worldly possessions, while Emily lifted a sleepy Carmen into her arms.

"Come on, honey," she murmured into the child's dark hair. "We're home now."

"Hey, hey, hey!" Helga howled, struggling to emerge from the confines of Ty's snug back seat. "I thought I warned you not to screw up my stuff!" Bursting out of the car, she hustled around to where Ty was grappling with tons of dirty plastic and shoved him out of the way. "Not like that, you knucklehead! What are ya trying to do?"

Wondering what the normally amiable Helga was up to, Emily gently pulled her out from under Tyler's impatient feet.

"What are you doing?" Emily chided, her brow drawn into a worried frown.

"Seeing what he's made of." Helga grinned at her and winked. "Thought I'd test him out a little bit. Make sure he's a nice guy."

"Well, tone it down a little, will you? We need to get some medicine for Carmen."

"Killjoy," Helga muttered, her eyes twinkling with mischief.

His starched white shirt was somewhat the worse for wear as Ty marched over to Emily, indignation written all over his face.

"Is she always like this?" he demanded, and plunged his hands through his corporate haircut, giving himself a cute, disheveled look.

Emily, now able to stand and really watch him in action, was again struck by how appealing he was. There was something vulnerable behind that big-business facade he presented to the world. Something tenderhearted and loving.

"No," she replied, biting back a smile. "Sometimes she's worse."

"Great. Just great," he muttered under his breath. "Roxanne's gonna love this. Come on, I'll show you to your room."

Roxanne? Of course. Why hadn't she thought of it before? He was married. Obviously to someone named Roxanne. Fighting a fanciful wave of melancholy, she took Carmen by the hand and led her into the house. What difference could it make that he was married? He wasn't really a knight in shining armor. Besides, she was here to get help for her two friends, not play the part of damsel in distress.

And what about Will? She was already interested in a man back home. Will Spencer, the man she'd been working for this summer as a nanny—that is, until the university had requested her research results three months early. Will thought she was still there, performing her job. And she was—in the form of her identical twin sister. She wondered how Erica was faring up there in Harvest Valley, posing as her. Probably just fine. It wasn't as if Will had ever paid that much attention to her. Her infatuation with him had always been one-sided. No, most likely Will hadn't even noticed the difference. It was kind of funny how she hadn't really thought much about him since she'd left.

Tugging on her hand, Carmen skipped into the house, chattering a mile a minute. *"La casa es muy, muy, muy bonita!"* she chirped happily, sneezing several times in quick succession, as she stared at the interior of Ty's opulent home in openmouthed awe.

Emily had to admit that, even though it was clear from the packing crates stacked in tidy piles that Ty was still moving in, his home was awesome. Carmen was right. This house was California living at its best.

Ty stopped and stared. "What's wrong with her?"

"She has a virus of some sort, I think."

"No. I mean, why is she talking that way?"

"You mean, Spanish?"

"Spanish?" Ty moaned. "She speaks *Spanish?*"

"Well, she *is* Mexican."

"Oh, great." He slapped his forehead with an open palm and muttered again under his breath. "A Spanish-speaking daughter. That's rich. Roxanne will probably just die laughing."

What was this about a daughter? Emily wondered, tightening her grip on Carmen's little hand. This man and his wife wanted a daughter? She didn't know who this Roxanne woman was, but she certainly didn't sound like mother material.

Ty was still staring in shock at Carmen. "Never mind," he finally grumbled. "I didn't get where I am today by not being able to figure out a problem as simple as a foreign language." Again he tore through his hair with frenzied hands. "You say she has a virus of some sort?" he asked, his hands suddenly stilling in his now-spiky hair.

Trying not to stare at the havoc he'd wreaked on his head, Emily met his eyes and saw genuine concern there. "I don't know, exactly. Late last night she had a temperature. At least, she felt warm to me. She's been sneezing and coughing for several days, and I'm afraid that if she doesn't get some antibiotics, it could get a lot worse."

Tyler rubbed his chin thoughtfully. "We've got a company doctor at Connstarr who will make house calls for employees. As soon as I get you settled, I'll give him a call."

"Thanks." Emily sighed as Carmen sleepily rubbed her eyes. Glancing at a fabulous antique clock standing just beneath the impressive staircase, she could see that it was already getting late in the evening. Fretting nervously, she wondered if the company doctor would be able to take a look at Carmen after 7:00 p.m. She wouldn't be able to sleep a wink until she knew the child would be all right. This time Carmen's stomach made its presence known, and the girl smiled shyly up at Tyler.

"That pizza will be here soon," he said, grinning as he mounted the stairs just off the massive tile-and-mahogany foyer. "Come on. All the bedrooms are up here."

Before he'd gone three steps, the front door burst open
and Helga strong-armed her plastic junkyard into his im-
peccable vestibule. "Which way?" she hollered, glancing
around curiously at her new surroundings.

Emily could tell that Helga was suitably impressed, by the
way she adjusted her plastic poncho and stood a little
straighter.

Grimacing, Tyler looked from her fully loaded shopping
cart to the stairs and back to the cart again. "This way." He
sighed, and, giving Helga a hand, led his three new house-
guests to their quarters.

"What the hell is she doing in there?" Tyler demanded,
three extra-large pizzas with the works balanced precari-
ously in his arms.

Emily nudged him out of Helga's room into the hallway
and closed the door after them. "She's, uh, nesting," she
explained, trying to defend Helga's eccentric behavior.

"Nesting?" he asked incredulously, his jaw hanging open.
"What for? She has a brand-new queen-size nest with fit-
ted sheets right there in the middle of the room. What does
she need that screwball tent for?"

"For the past few years it's been her only protection from
the elements. Kind of like a child's security blanket. She's
just used to it, that's all. It's okay. Really. She's not dangerous or anything," she assured him, and looked long-
ingly at the boxes he held.

"Well . . ." He glanced doubtfully back at Helga's door
and sighed. She was part of the deal. He guessed he'd just
figure out a way to cope with it. A lunatic for a mother-in-
law and a daughter who didn't speak English. Roxanne was
going to have a field day. "Dinner's served. Grab the kid
and the kook, and join me in the kitchen. You and I can talk
about your new duties after we get some food in your stomach." He sounded a little gruffer than he'd intended.

She looked so grateful, he felt guilty about making an issue over the mess in Helga's room. What was it about her that turned his guts to mush every time she favored him with her warm, caring smile?

Emily had never tasted such delicious pizza. She could feel Ty watching her as she ravenously devoured an entire pie all by herself. The only person who ate faster and with more gusto was Helga.

"You gonna eat that?" The older woman eyed a half-eaten crust on Ty's plate.

"No. No...go ahead."

"Thanks." Helga stuffed his leftovers into her mouth and winked at Emily.

Emily had to admit that she admired the way Ty handled Helga. The old woman had been putting him through his paces all through dinner, and slowly but surely his boyish charm was winning the old woman over.

"Yap," Helga said as she got up from the table. "I'll put my friend Carmen here to bed. It's way past her bedtime," she explained, and hoisted a sleepy but satisfied Carmen into her arms.

"Thanks, Helga. Good night..." Emily called after her, her plastic poncho rustling as she moved quickly out of the room.

As she turned toward Tyler she could still feel his probing eyes following her every move. She smiled self-consciously, wondering if she had added pizza sauce to the grime on her face. A nervous twitch settled into the corner of her mouth and she squirmed uncomfortably in her chair. She still had no idea what this man expected of her.

In a effort to break the ice, she decided to thank him for having the doctor over so promptly. She felt much better knowing that the child was all right.

"Thanks," she began tentatively as she wiped her hands with a paper napkin. "The doctor says that Carmen will be fine. She just had a touch of the flu. He says she's nearly over it. I didn't know doctors still made house calls," she rambled, wishing she knew why he was watching her so closely.

Ty smiled. "I'm glad she's going to be okay, because tomorrow is going to be a busy day for all of us," he said, wadding up his own napkin and tossing it onto his plate. He leaned back in his chair and rubbed his hand across his jaw. Correctly reading her quizzical expression, he said, "You're wondering why I brought you here."

"Yes." Fear, mingled with excitement, tiptoed down her spine.

"Good question." He sighed and studied her face critically. He looked up at the ceiling for a moment. "Why...did I bring you here?" He repeated the question, as though trying to figure out the answer himself. "Well..." He moved forward in his seat and regarded her seriously. "To put it simply, I brought you here because I need a wife."

Chapter Three

"A wife?"

"In a word, yes."

Tyler could tell that he'd knocked her for a loop. He knew how she felt. This morning he'd gotten up and gone to work, a single, unencumbered, carefree bachelor. This evening he'd come home with three wacky new family members who were already turning his apple-pie-order life upside down.

His house was suddenly a mess, Helga was only playing with half a deck, and the child barely spoke any English. Not to mention the fact that their strange behavior was giving him a heart attack.

The only hope he had of turning these unlikely crew members into the family of his dreams, was the woman seated in front of him. The woman who sat there now, looking at him as if he'd lost his mind.

"As in, till death do us part?" Her eyes were round as dinner platters.

"No, no, no." Ty chuckled uneasily. She didn't have to look so repulsed. Lots of women thought he was a pretty decent catch. "Only for a weekend."

"A weekend?" she squeaked.

"Or two," he amended.

"You need a *weekend wife?*"

"Ah, yes, and...probably some weekdays in between, too...."

Tyler studied her horrified face, while trying to think of a way to explain this whole thing gracefully. He couldn't lose her now. Not this one. If he could just get her to agree to go along with him, he had a feeling that she would be perfect.

Before the pizza had arrived and while the company doctor was looking in on Carmen, he'd called the local shopping mall and made some appointments at the hairdresser's for them. Fashion makeovers weren't his bag, but the guy at Maxime's Impressionistic Hair should know his stuff. What the heck? Couldn't hurt. By the end of the day tomorrow, hopefully they wouldn't recognize themselves. Hopefully *he* wouldn't recognize them, either.

Although, he mused, even layers of dirt and grime couldn't hide the classic structure of her face. Tearing his eyes away from the fear he saw etched in her expression, he took a deep breath and decided to plunge in.

"Actually, I—"

The phone rang.

Damn it anyway. He smiled apologetically at her. "That's the phone in my office, so I know it's work related. I'd...better get it. I'll probably be a while, so please, make yourself at home. I promise to tell you everything as soon as I'm finished."

Nodding dumbly, Emily watched him go. He wanted her to be his wife, this weekend? And next? And the days in between? What did that mean? Shivering violently at the ugly thoughts that tumbled through her brain, she pushed herself away from the table and ran upstairs on wobbly legs. She told herself she needed to check on Carmen. However, if she were honest, she knew what she really wanted was to check on him. Maybe if she poked around for a while upstairs, she could find some sort of clue as to who—or what—he was. Normal men did not propose marriage to women they found at the side of the road.

Carmen was sleeping like an angel. It looked like Helga had managed to wipe Carmen's face and hands before popping her into her first comfortable bed in ages. Her cheeks, scrubbed pink, lay against freshly laundered, lace-edged pillowcases, and her tiny rosebud mouth was pulled into a smile that spoke of pleasant dreams.

Peeking in across the hall, Emily was glad to see Helga snoring away atop Ty's large guest bed. The cockamamy tent she'd constructed, just for appearances, was forsaken in favor of a firm mattress.

It broke her heart, now that she knew Ty was a madman, that by this time tomorrow night they'd be back out on the street. Even though he didn't seem dangerous so far, she couldn't take any chances. Shutting the door softly, she tiptoed down the hallway and wondered where to begin sleuthing for clues to this guy's character. She was seriously thinking about turning him in to the authorities.

The master suite seemed like the most logical place to start.

Ty's large, airy bedroom had that just-unpacked feel. Empty boxes were stacked in a corner, and large, framed pictures leaned against the wall waiting to be hung. The windows still needed curtains, but Emily could tell that when this room was finished it would be fantastic. Across the room, French doors led to a veranda that looked out over the pool area. Next to that, an open archway led to an enormous master bath, done in gleaming chrome, crystal and brass.

What she wouldn't give for a bath in this, she thought, running a hand over the whirlpool tub's smooth, marble surface. Two could probably fit in this tub with room to spare—

What the heck was she thinking? Daydreaming about taking a bath with that...that...lunatic downstairs? *Get a grip.*

Glancing up, she spotted her reflection in the mirror and was horrified by what she saw. She hadn't checked her appearance in well over a week, and it was clear that outdoor living did not agree with her regular beauty regime.

Her once luxurious, silky, shiny, golden brown hair now hung in greasy strings at the sides of her face. And the face. Gaunt and drawn were two words that came to mind as she took in her sallow complexion. She looked like a chimney sweep.

The clothes that had fit perfectly when she'd started this project now hung in filthy tatters on her slender frame. It was amazing what a week or so of eating beans could do for those excess curves, she thought.

Unable to stand the dirt and grime for another second, Emily quickly strode to the inviting walk-in shower and turned on the hot water. This would only take a second, she decided, stripping out of her grubby clothes and tossing them onto the floor. Besides, hadn't he said for her to make herself at home? Hopefully he would stay on the phone for a few more minutes.

Glorious hot water cascaded over her head. Loading her hair with scented shampoo, Emily lathered it into a mountain of suds. Oh, how wonderful the warm, penetrating spray felt on her shoulders and back as she ran the soapy washcloth over her frame. She scrubbed at her flesh until she could feel it squeak with cleanliness, then rinsed her hair thoroughly and shut off the faucet. Grabbing a huge, fluffy bath sheet, she hurriedly dried off and wrapped it around herself. She found a brand-new toothbrush in his medicine cabinet and brushed her teeth.

Looking down at her filthy pile of rags in dismay, she decided that there was no way she could put her clothes back on until they'd been washed. Tyler probably wouldn't mind if she borrowed some of his clothes. Anyway, at this point, she didn't really care what he thought of her.

Tiptoeing into his bedroom, she discovered one of his dress shirts hanging over a bedpost. It would do for now. Donning it, she rolled the sleeves up to her elbows and was glad to discover that it covered her somewhat modestly.

Fear that Ty would probably come looking for her as soon as he finished his business on the phone had her nerves jangling as she tried to button his shirt with shaky fingers. When she was halfway done, she knew she'd missed a hole and gave up. No time.

After a rapid search of his dresser drawers, she finally found his underwear and pulled out a pair of silly boxers sporting dancing pickles. They would have to do. Pulling them on, she plunged her hands deeper into his tidy drawer and groped around for a pair of socks.

He was a bit of a neat-nick, she noted, quite unlike herself. She had always felt that orderly drawers were the sign of a boring mind. Well, Tyler Newroth blew that theory all to heck. With his intense good looks and that powerful build, not to mention his insane ideas about marriage, Ty was anything but boring. No, most certainly not . . . boring.

What on earth was this? Pushing aside a pile of socks, Emily was stunned to find a bottle of champagne wrapped in what looked like lacy women's underwear and tied with— *handcuffs?*

Was *this* the proposal he'd had in mind? Well, he could just take her back to the freeway where he'd found her. She was no man's terminator, or dominator, or whatever the heck it was one did with handcuffs and the like. No, thank you. If he wanted to wear women's undies, he'd have to do it on his own time.

Her heart thundered fearsomely in her ears as she lifted the handcuffs off the bottle and let them dangle from her fingertips. Why would he seek her out? She had neither the looks nor the talent for this type of thing. And how on earth would she ever fit *this* juicy tidbit into her thesis?

No way. She'd better grab Helga and Carmen and make a run for it. Now. If she were lucky, they could all be back out on the highway before Ty could say "Spank me."

"I see you found my room."

"Argh!" Emily screamed, and whirled around. Handcuffs in hand, she faced Ty, who stood squarely in his doorway, watching her.

Ohmagoshohmagosh. Her heart bounced around in her rib cage, building centrifugal force and threatening to burst out of her chest. Her entire body quaked with terror, and she had to will herself not to faint. "I... Ha...uh... I—I—" she stuttered, so fearfully it began to make her angry.

Why was she on trial here? He was the pervert. And she was probably his next victim!

"Yeah!" Her body shook with rage. "I sure did!" she snapped, launching the handcuffs—bottle of champagne and all—in his direction. "And that's not all I found!"

"What the...?" Ty gasped as he dodged the bottle just before it hit the doorframe and exploded. "What the hell are you doing?"

Emily crouched low, looking for a way to escape and keep his shirt closed over the dancing-pickle boxers at the same time. If she had to, she'd leap over the veranda into the pool. Then, if she didn't drown, she'd run for help.

"If you think just because you picked me up on the freeway, that you can handcuff me and play...*kinky sex games,* you're sadly mistaken, bucko!" she shrieked, her eyes wild.

Ty ran his hands through his hair in exasperation. Bucko? Her reaction to Roxanne's gift seemed a little prissy in light of the fact that she was a street person. How on earth had she found the damn thing in the first place? He'd stashed it in his underwear drawer, for crying out loud....

Ah. His eyes swept over her slender body, clad only in his dress shirt and boxers. She'd showered. And merciful mama, she cleaned up very nicely. She must have found it while looking for something to wear.

Glancing from her smooth, tanned thighs up to her face, he could see the gears turning in her brain. Ever so slowly, she began to back toward the French doors that led to the veranda. What on earth was she doing?

Moving farther into the room, Ty said, "I don't think you should go out there..."

"Don't come near me!" she warned, her voice deadly.

"Hey, now. Wait a minute. You've got it all wrong here." Ty stepped farther into the room toward her.

"Stop!" she cried, clutching his shirt closed across her breasts as she worked her way to the doors.

Ty glanced out to the veranda. If she thought she could make it to the pool from up here, she was sadly mistaken, he thought worriedly. It was much farther than it looked. Not wanting to add scraping a dead body off his patio to his already totally bad day, he decided to stop her.

He hadn't been his university's starting quarterback for nothing. Bolting across the room, he cut her off at the pass, lifted her lithe and wriggling body into his arms and tackled her on the bed. Her howls of terror could wake the dead.

"Shh! You'll wake up the kid!" he rasped as, tired of trying to convince her to shut up, he covered her mouth with his hand. "Ouch!" he yelped when she bit down hard. Jerking his hand away from her face, he examined it for blood. "What'd you do that for?"

"Get off me, you pervert!" she grunted, struggling like a wild animal beneath his powerful body.

However, Ty, being more experienced in contact sports, held her firmly in place by throwing a leg over her flailing limbs and pinning her arms down next to her sides.

"Now hang on just a minute here! You've got this all wrong! *Ouch!* Damn it!" He groaned and clutched his lower midsection where her knee had connected with one of his more vulnerable areas. "Would you knock it off? I'm trying to explain... *Uff!*"

Good heavens, she was a wildcat. Lucky thing he'd never run up against her in a football game. He'd never have stood a chance, he thought sourly as he pulled her fingers out of his nose and eyes.

Man, oh, man, she was a slippery devil, and she fought dirty. It was all he could do to keep her legs from knocking him senseless. He lunged at her ankles as she escaped from beneath him and crawled like a crab, hell-bent for water, to the edge of the bed.

"Will you just *chill out?*" he gasped, lurching after her as she slithered off the bed. *"Ow!* Hey! That hurt!" he yelped as she reached up and clobbered him in the eye with his alarm clock.

"Why, you surprise me," she grunted sarcastically, trying to free her ankle from his death grip. "I thought you sex fiends were into pain!" Flailing her arms like a windmill in a hurricane, she proceeded to send his lamp crashing to the floor, along with the contents of his nightstand.

"Oh, for the love of—" No wonder she was homeless. She'd probably torn her home down. And, at the rate she was going, he'd be out on the street with her in no time. "I've been trying to tell you... I'm not a pervert!" he roared, hauling her back up onto the bed next to him.

"Sure!" she yelled. "Just don't get into an accident. The doctor might not understand your taste in underwear!" Rolling over to the opposite side of the bed, she kicked his other nightstand over.

Growing infinitely weary of her American Gladiator act, Ty decided he'd had enough. He couldn't begin to imagine what his neighbors must be thinking. "Shut up!" he growled. *"Now!"* He clamped his hand back over her mouth and hoped she wouldn't bite again.

Looking down into her fear-filled, liquid brown eyes, he shook his head and exhaled heavily. She was terrified and he didn't blame her. But he had to admire her spunk. Something about this little spitfire turned him on.

"I'm not going to hurt you. Honest." He didn't know what else he could say to convince her.

Exhausted, he sank down on the bed next to her, his hand still firmly pressed against her soft lips. Oh, man, he groaned inwardly. She smelled good. She felt good. She looked good. He drew his eyes away from his dancing-pickle boxers and over his misbuttoned dress shirt to her eyes.

Even though Ty wished he could lie here with his nose buried in her soft, sweet-smelling hair all night, he knew he had some explaining to do. Propping himself up on one elbow beside her, he asked, "Will you be quiet now?"

He felt her quick and silent nod beneath his hand, and slowly pulled his fingers from their firm grip over her mouth.

"That's better." He sighed, collapsing on his back next to her. "Now then. If you'll promise to shut up and hear my side of the story, I'll let you up," he said.

As she nodded again, he lifted his leg from across her body and sat up, pulling her with him. She was frantically tugging at the shirt she wore, trying to cover the delicious dips and curves that still had his blood pounding in his ears.

"Here," he said, pushing off the bed and striding to his dresser. Pulling out a pair of running shorts with a drawstring and some white sport socks, he tossed them over at her and ordered gruffly, "Put these on and meet me downstairs in the living room. I promise I'll explain everything. If you don't like what I have to offer you, you're free to go whenever you like. And," he added, stepping gingerly over the broken champagne bottle on his way out the door, "watch out for broken glass."

Ty ran down to the kitchen and pulled a bottle of brandy out of a cabinet. He needed a drink. Totally thunderstruck by the difference in her appearance, he pondered how amazing it was that a simple shower could transform someone so completely. He was still reeling from the impact of their wrestling match on his bed.

She was incredible. Fiery, passionate, beautiful. And those legs. Slender, shapely legs that seemed to go on forever. He just *had* to convince her to stay. With that sweet, innocent face and those huge, sparkly brown eyes, his heart leapt with excitement. All she needed was the right clothes and hair, and this woman could give Roxanne a run for her money anyday. If he could only get her to cooperate.

For some reason, he had the feeling that under her false wall of bravado, she was a lady. Somewhere along the way— before something had gone terribly wrong—Ty was sure that she'd lived a much better life.

Sensing that Ty was watching her from the doorway, Emily ran an anxious hand over the outfit she'd borrowed from him. She was probably a first-class fool for sitting here, waiting for him to fill her head with lies, but she couldn't help herself. There had been something sincere about his promise to explain. And, for the life of her, she just couldn't make herself leave. Yet.

Plus, she guessed she owed it to Helga and Carmen to hear him out. What if he was a nice person? She pulled her lower lip into her mouth. He wasn't that nice. And what about that kinky pile of stuff she'd found in his drawer?

No, she would definitely be on her guard with this guy.

"Can I get you something to drink?" he asked, carrying a bottle into the room with him.

"No, thank you," she said primly, she'd keep her wits about her, thank you very much. She was surprised and embarrassed to note that he had the beginnings of a first-class shiner.

Ty set the bottle on the wet bar. "Now then..." He cleared his throat. "Where were we?" Crossing the room, he sank down onto the couch opposite hers.

Fighting like a pair of mad dogs? "Till death do us part." She hoped her accusing glare made him nervous.

"Oh, yes." He smiled tiredly at her sardonic expression. "I should probably start at the beginning. And if you'll just bear with me, I'll explain everything. Even the handcuffs."

At her slight nod, he continued.

"As I told you earlier, I just moved to L.A. from Boston. I was transferred and promoted to the position of director of national accounts at Connstarr. Connstarr is one of the nation's leading software companies. Computers," he explained, as though she wouldn't know what software was.

Bristling, she rolled her eyes and nodded. She may be homeless, but she wasn't stupid.

Leaning forward in his seat, his expression hardened. "I worked my way through college, then started at the bottom at Connstarr. It has taken me over ten long years to get where I am today. I fought to get there. I'll fight to stay there. That's where you come in." His eyes glittered dangerously.

"Me?" Suddenly curious to find out how she fit into the scheme of things, Emily forgot her animosity for a moment.

"Yes. You."

"How?"

"Ever since I started my new job in the L.A. office, I have been ... er, u-uh ..." he stammered, wondering how to put it. "Harassed."

"Harassed?" She lifted a skeptical brow.

"Sexually."

"*Sexually?*" Her lip curled in disbelief. A big, strong guy like him? Who was he trying to kid?

Flames of embarrassment licked at his cheeks.

"I know. It's hard to swallow. I don't quite believe it myself. But it's true." Standing, he strode to the wet bar in the corner, poured himself a brandy, and held the cool glass against his darkening eye. "Are you sure you don't want anything?"

"I'm sure."

"Anyway..." He took a slug of his drink and leaned against the bar. "Roxanne Delmonico—that's my new boss," he said derisively, "has it in her head that she... Aw, jeez..." He took a deep breath. "Wants me." He dragged his hand over his face and glanced over at her as if he was worried about her reaction.

"So, Roxanne isn't your wife," she murmured.

"No," he answered, surprised. "Whatever gave you that idea?"

"I thought you said something about her wanting a daughter that didn't speak Spanish."

"Oh, that. I'll get to that." He shook his head. "Normally, I wouldn't have any problem dealing with a situation like this, but unfortunately for me, she's the owner's niece."

Emily snorted. "That figures," she muttered to herself.

Ty shot her a curious look. "Uncle Denny Delmonico." His words held a certain fondness. "Nicest guy you'd ever want to meet. Too nice. He's totally blind when it comes to his spoiled, man-eating niece. He gave her the vice presidency of the West Coast division of Connstarr last year. And she's been terrorizing the troops ever since."

Pushing off the bar, Ty ambled over and sat down across from Emily. "She is the one who sent the handcuffs and other stuff you found. It was my Welcome to L.A. gift from the boss. Classy, huh?"

Emily's mouth hung open in amazement. She'd had a professor who'd pulled the same kind of chicanery with her last year. If Ty was telling the truth, she knew how infuriating it could be. Especially when the harasser in question held your future in their hands.

"I thought I might keep the stuff you found as evidence, if I ever need to build a case against her."

Emily looked contritely at her hands.

Tossing back the rest of his drink, he sighed and set his tumbler down on the coffee table. "This morning," he began tiredly, "Roxanne came into my office and asked me if I'd received her gift. Then she suggested that we try it out this weekend."

Emily leaned forward as curiosity got the better of her. "What does she look like?"

Ty squeezed his eyes tightly shut and rubbed his forehead. "Blond, bold, buxom, brassy, and a few other *B* words I'm too polite to mention in front of a lady." Opening his eyes, he looked seriously at her. "She's blackmailing me with my future. If I don't come across, or find a damn good reason not to, she'll fire me. She's done it before."

Emily drew in a quick breath.

Suddenly Ty stood. "Do you want some ice cream? I'm still feeling a little peckish." He grinned boyishly.

"No wonder. We didn't leave you much pizza." Before she could stop herself, she returned his grin. "Sure. Ice cream sounds fine."

"Hang on a sec. I'll be right back."

Watching him bound out of the room, Emily closed her eyes and sighed. Maybe it was crazy, but she was beginning to believe him. Something about Tyler Newroth appealed to her, and for some reason, against her better judgment, she trusted him. He was certainly handsome enough for it to be plausible. Roxanne's admiration was not groundless. Just unprofessional. And illegal.

"Hope you like rum raisin," he said, jogging back into the room and handing her a small carton with a spoon sticking out.

"My favorite."

"Really?" His eyes darted curiously to hers. "Mine, too."

Why that should please her, she'd never know. There was something interesting about him that she had never reacted to with any other man before. Yes, she thought uncomfortably, there was definitely a certain chemistry of sorts going on here, whether she wanted to admit it or not.

"So, what did you say when she asked you to try out her little gift?" she asked over a mouthful of ice cream.

"I tried to stall her the best I could. But if you knew Roxanne, you'd know that she doesn't take no for an answer. She actually crawled up onto my desk—lay on a project I was working on—and told me I needed to loosen up."

His laugh was incredulous. "She said she wanted to get to know me *much* better." He wiggled his eyebrows up and down suggestively.

"Hmm . . . I wonder what she meant by that?" Her voice dripped with sarcasm.

"I wonder." Ty shook his spoon at her.

"So, how'd you get her off your desk?"

"I told her I was married."

"Are you?"

"No."

"Did she believe you?"

"I don't think so." His face was crestfallen as he scooped another bite of ice cream into his mouth.

Even though Tyler Newroth was not a man to be pitied, and he was far from the underdog, Emily's heart began to melt at his plight. Women all over this country were being sexually harassed every single day. It was unconscionable. So why should the standard be any different for a man?

Her desire, however, to help this man was not her usual bleeding-heart project. No. This was different. She didn't know why exactly. Maybe it was the fact that Helga and Carmen's futures, as well as his, rested on her willingness to help.

"In fact," he said, swallowing a big spoonful of ice cream, "she pretty much laughed at me. Then, before she left the office, she reminded me about the company cruise."

"Cruise?"

"Connstarr is treating its entire management staff and their families to a week-long Mexican cruise, a week from Monday."

"Uh-oh." Emily could see where this was going and swallowed nervously. She sincerely hoped he didn't expect her to get on a boat. In the water. Out in the middle of the ocean. The very thought made her stomach churn.

"Uh-oh is right. On her way out the door she said, all phony and gushylike, 'Looking forward to meeting your wife.'" Ty smirked. "Then she has the nerve to insinuate that we'll find some time alone together on the ship, behind the little woman's back."

"She sounds like a real pistol."

Ty laughed ruefully. "Bingo. On the way home from work, she calls me on my car phone and invites me to this big-deal client meeting with Uncle Denny and herself. I tell her, sure, I'll be there. Then she tells me that the client is a real family guy and wants to meet my wife. This coming Monday!" He snorted. "Well, she correctly suspects I don't have a wife. And since I just moved here last week, I don't even have a girlfriend yet. And I may have a way with Roxanne, but I doubt that I'm charming enough to con some stranger into pretending to be my wife by Monday evening."

Perhaps he underestimated himself, Emily mused, amazed at how "at home" she felt now, sitting here in his clothes and eating ice cream. Too "at home," she thought uneasily. She couldn't let herself start to feel sorry for this guy.

"So I thought I'd try hiring someone." Ty scraped the bottom of his carton and, after getting the last bit of ice cream, dropped the empty container on the coffee table. Leaning back on the couch, he propped his feet up next to the carton and smiled at her. "That's when I spotted you. Your sign said Will Work For Food. So... how was the ice cream?" he asked, the brandy and his unexpected workout with her causing his eyelids to droop appealingly.

"Delicious, so I guess I owe you." Finishing off her ice cream, she dropped her container into his and tossed her spoon down on the coffee table.

She sighed heavily and realized that she truly believed his story. And, unfortunately, Emily could never resist a challenge. Besides, it would be a pretty cushy way to get help for Carmen and Helga—except for the part about the ocean. But is that what she wanted? An easy way out? What would this experience do to her findings? Then again, what difference did her findings make if Helga and Carmen were out suffering on the street?

Eyeing him skeptically, she asked, "You really think we could pull it off?"

"I'm not sure." He shook his head. "I've done everything else I can think of, short of telling her to take her job and shove it."

"What about Helga and Carmen?"

"What about them?"

"They're part of the deal. Where I go, they go." Carmen had been through far too much upheaval in her short life to be abandoned again. And Helga wasn't as strong as she let on.

Ty shrugged. "Well, if that's the only way I can have you, then I'll take them."

"On the cruise?"

"Sure. Whatever." His lip curled in wry amusement. "Helga can be the mother-in-law, and Carmen can be the daughter."

"What about Carmen's language problem?"

"We'll say we decided to adopt."

He had an answer for just about everything. She had to admire that. It was then that she realized she had just agreed to pose as this man's wife on a cruise ship in front of the entire Connstarr management team. Obviously a man and his wife would share a cabin. And after what had happened earlier on his bed . . .

She had a feeling she'd be fighting him again. Fighting an attraction to him that she'd felt from the moment he'd saved her neck at the side of the road.

She nibbled nervously on her lower lip. "What about the sleeping arrangements?"

Ty grinned. "What do you have in mind?"

Unable to miss the teasing gleam in his eye, Emily pursed her lips. "I'll sleep with the girls on the ship."

"Don't you think Roxanne will wonder why a married couple would sleep in separate cabins?"

It was a valid point, she knew. "I guess I could go to your cabin for appearances, and then, when the coast is clear, scoot over to their cabin."

"Works for me." Ty smiled easily. "Does this mean you'll take the job?"

"If you'll feed us and get us medicine when we need it, then, yes, I'll help you."

"I'd do that anyway."

Emily believed he would.

He toyed anxiously for a moment with the pillow at his side. "Uh, Emily..."

"Yes?"

"I told her we were newlyweds. High school sweethearts. She thinks we decided to tie the knot just before I moved out here."

"Oh?"

"Yeah. My file says I'm single, so she has to think it just happened. I...just wanted to let you know. So that we can...act like...you know..."

"Newlyweds?"

"Yeah," he breathed, clearly embarrassed. "You know, sort of, well, lovey-dovey."

Just what did he have in mind? Emily wondered. Surely no passionate public displays of affection. Probably just a little hand-holding here and there. She would do the best she could, and keep her emotions out of it. If the job required a little "newlywed" behavior on her part, well, then she'd do it. For Carmen. For Helga. And she'd stay emotionally detached. She glanced up at his hopeful, boyish face. Well, she'd try, anyway.

Before she knew she'd opened her mouth, she found herself agreeing. "Okay. You're hiring me to be your new bride, I'll be your new bride. In public we're, uh, lovey-dovey. In private, we're just, um, employer and employee."

He was visibly relieved. "Terrific. I promise to be a perfect gentleman," he said, and grinned. "What about Helga? Do you think she'll go along with it?"

"Helga is a good sport. I think as long as you treat her fairly, she'll do the same for you."

"Great. And Carmen?"

"Carmen will love you."

"Okay, then." He extended his hand across the coffee table. "Deal?"

Emily knew she was probably in way over her head here, but since when had that ever stopped her from rushing in where angels feared to tread?

"Deal." She returned his strong, warm grip. A grip that he held a fraction longer than necessary before he let it drop.

"Emily?"

"Hmm?" For the first time in days, she felt as if she could truly relax. Settling back on Tyler's big, overstuffed couch, she curled her legs up underneath her and studied his curious face.

"How is it that you three came to be standing on the freeway together today?"

He was fishing for information. Information she couldn't give him if she were to maintain the integrity of her thesis. The idea was to be homeless. Completely homeless. That meant not telling anyone, for a solid month, about her research project. It meant living the life as if she had no other choice. As much as she longed to confide in Ty that she wasn't some poor, wandering soul, she couldn't. She was in it too deep to break the rules now. Maybe someday she could tell him the truth. Till then, she was homeless. At his mercy.

"We needed to eat," she said evasively.

"I got that much." He smiled. "I mean, what happened to bring the three of you together in the first place? Why are you all living on the street?"

That was a good question. One she wished she knew the answer to. One she hoped her project could help answer in some small way.

"Well..." She decided to be truthful up to a point. "Carmen's mother and father died last winter of TB."

"Really?"

"Believe it or not, in this day and age." She shook her head sadly. "And Helga's husband committed suicide several years ago, leaving her penniless. She had nowhere to go.

"I found them huddled together under a freeway overpass a while ago. Some gang members had been hassling me, and Helga offered me refuge in her tent." She shivered at the memory. If it hadn't been for Helga's kooky street smarts, Emily was sure she'd have been killed. She owed the old woman her life, and vowed to get her off the streets if it was the last thing she ever did.

"What about you?" he asked gently. "How did you end up out on the streets?"

"Me?" Emily laughed. "I'm not that interesting, I'm afraid. Just...ran out of luck, I guess." Wanting to take the spotlight off herself, she said, "Thank you for taking us in. You don't know what your help means to me."

"I could say the same to you." He flashed her a relieved and happy smile.

"Well, I don't know about that. But I will promise to hold up my end of the bargain." Her face grew quite serious as she stood. "As if my life depended on it."

Looking at her curiously, he also stood and walked with her to the stairs. "Me, too," he said, and knew that it was true.

Just before mounting the stairs, she smiled and whispered, "Good night."

"'Night," he called after her as he watched her go, his shirt teasing her graceful legs as she danced up the stairs.

Friday, July 22. Late evening.
Dear Diary:
My study has suddenly taken a left turn. I don't know

if this is good or bad yet. However, I have decided to see where this change of events takes us.

I wanted to maintain the integrity of this study by being as authentic as possible and, so far, I have lived the life. I can only surmise that if I were truly homeless, and Tyler Newroth had seen me at the side of the road, I would be here anyway. However, I can't help but wonder what I will learn about being homeless from the deck of a cruise ship. Hopefully it will all come together.

So, I will see where this experience takes us, and continue to pray that eventually Helga and Carmen will find homes of their own. As far as I can tell, Ty seems like a good man. I've decided to trust him, and feel that we can maintain a working relationship of sorts, even though I'm sure some aspects of our ruse will be awkward.

Chapter Four

"Good morning."

"Good morning." Ty looked out from behind his morning edition of the *Times*, to find Emily standing uncertainly in the dining room doorway. Still damp from her morning shower, she looked as lovely as a rose, clad only in his white terry-cloth robe. She had a bundle of dirty laundry tucked under her arm.

"I hope you don't mind." She smiled warily, glancing down at his robe. "It was hanging in the guest bathroom."

"No. That's fine." Ty folded his paper and motioned for her to join him at the breakfast table. "I haven't hired a cook yet, so I'm afraid it's just cereal this morning."

"Cereal will be fine." The way her eyes swept over the half-dozen different kinds of cereal on the table told him that it was more than all right with her. But still, she made no move to sit down.

"Where are Helga and Carmen?" he asked, glancing behind her. He'd have thought Helga would have plowed through several bowls, including his, by now.

"Actually—" she shifted her eyes to the load she held in her arms "—they're upstairs taking a bath. I was wondering if you'd mind if I popped our clothes into your washer, while they bathe. These are Carmen's and mine. Helga wears mainly plastic, so..."

"Sure. No problem." Ty hopped up from the table and led Emily back to his laundry room. Too bad there was no pot-scrubber setting on his clothes washer, he mused as he poured twice the recommended amount of detergent into his machine, and stuffed in the filthy, tattered garments. "What do you want to do about Helga's clothes? I have a garden hose out back," he suggested teasingly.

Emily laughed. "Well, for the time being, if you had another bathrobe, she could wear that till we figure out what she wants."

"Sure. Just look in my closet." At her dubious expression, he chuckled easily. "Don't worry," he said joshingly, "I keep the whips and chains in the garage."

"That's a relief." She smiled.

Her smile was radiant in the sunshine that streamed in through his laundry room window. She looked amazingly natural, standing there in his robe, her hair pulled into a loose ponytail. It was hard to believe that she'd been living on the street only yesterday. And yet she seemed so fresh and innocent and unscarred. He still couldn't believe his luck. Hopefully, Roxanne would never be able to doubt a face like this.

"Did you tell Helga about the cruise and everything?" Ty asked, and braced himself for the bad news. He had a feeling the old bird would pitch a fit, for some reason.

"Mmm-hmm."

"What'd she say?"

"Um ... I can't exactly repeat what she said, but I think she'll be okay. Eventually." Emily smiled at his dubious expression and reached out to give him a reassuring pat on the arm. "Don't worry. When I told her about all the food on a cruise ship, she wanted to know how soon we were going to leave."

Tyler rubbed at the knots between his shoulder blades. Sometimes he wondered if he'd have been better off forgoing his promotion and staying in Boston. No amount of money was worth this stress. Oh, well, since there was no way he would ever be able to control Helga, he might as well give up and relax. And, on the bright side, if she misbehaved too badly, it just might be his ticket back to Boston and away from Roxanne.

The washer had finished filling with hot water and was busy churning the dirt out of the pathetic rags it held.

Turning to leave the laundry room, Ty tucked his hand through Emily's arm and drew her into the hallway. "Luckily, we don't have to leave for over a week. But we have a lot to do before then. Why don't we talk about it over breakfast?" he suggested, and led Emily back to the dining room.

Maxime's Impressionistic Hair. How Tyler had managed to fast-talk them into this, Emily would never know. Yet, here they sat, all three of them, sacrificial lambs awaiting slaughter at the ring-encrusted hands of Maxime and his merry band of shampooers.

Helga had nearly sent Ty into a fit of apoplexy that morning at the breakfast table when she'd none-too-graciously declined his invitation to a day at the hairdresser's and the mall for a new wardrobe.

"If them stuck-up co-workers of yours don't like my hair, then they can just kiss my split ends!" she'd crabbed at the red-faced and flustered Ty. "I won't go one inch out of my way for that bunch of snobs. No, sir."

It wasn't until after breakfast that Emily was able to take her aside and convince her that it was in Carmen's best interest to go along with Ty's request.

"It sure is easy to get him all riled up," Helga had said with a grin after she'd grudgingly capitulated.

"Yes, and I notice that you go out of your way to do it," Emily'd admonished good-naturedly.

Helga had hooted. "He's kinda cute when he's all red in the face, don't you think?"

"I hadn't noticed."

"Sure. And I'm Mrs. Trump."

"Here." Pink-cheeked, Emily had thrust a pair of Ty's sweats at the impish woman. "Put these on."

With much pomp and circumstance, Helga had managed to squeeze her rotund figure into Ty's sweats, saying, "I like my men with a little more meat on their bones."

"He's not skinny."

"Really?" Helga had teasingly tweaked her on the nose. "And here I thought you hadn't noticed."

When they had arrived at the salon, Ty had handed Maxime his credit card and told him to "give them the works." Then the coward had turned tail and run, Emily fumed, as though the smell of the perm solution would somehow render him impotent.

The diamonds on Max's gigantic rings flashed as he ran his hands through her long, thick, satiny hair. "Oh, gad! This stuff is *gorgeous!* I would *kill* for hair like this! Ralph! Come here, man. Will you look at this hair? It's to *die* for!" Swirling his fingers through her luxurious hair, Emily watched Max in the mirror as his eyes rolled back into his head in ecstasy. "What would you do with it?" Max asked the expressionless Ralph.

"Cut it off." Casting an apathetic glance in her direction, Ralph shrugged and blew a stream of cigarette smoke at the ceiling.

"Yes! That's *exactly* what I was thinking!" Max shrieked in delight.

"Wha—" Emily gasped in horror, but was too late.

Max's expert shears flashed with the precision of a samurai's sword, and before she knew what hit her, her crowning glory landed in her lap.

"You can give that to lover boy as a souvenir," Max chortled before yanking her backward into the shampoo bowl.

Emily bit back the tears as Max shampooed and rinsed, snipped and clipped, permed and highlighted, styled and spritzed. It was all part of the experiment, she told herself, attempting to swallow past the thickening in her throat. Of course she could sacrifice her beautiful head of hair in the name of research. It was for a good cause.

Squeezing her eyes tightly closed, she tried to shut out Max's loud, flamboyant self-proclamations of genius, and wondered absently how Helga and Carmen were faring. Every so often, over the whine of a blow-dryer, she could hear the older woman's bawdy cackle as something would tickle her funny bone. At least someone here was having some fun, she thought grumpily.

"I *love* it!" Max, braying like a donkey, stood back and critically eyed his handiwork. "It's you, it's you, *it's you!* No, no. Don't look yet," he chided, spinning her chair away from the mirror. "I want you to get the full effect after Ralph has done your makeup. You're really lucky that he's here today. Usually he's out on some movie set, doing Michelle or Demi or Julia or *somebody.*" He winked conspiratorially at her.

While Ralph applied his rather passionless art to the canvas of her face, Emily wondered what was keeping Ty. Hopefully, he'd show up soon so that she could give him another black eye.

Ty slammed the door to his Mercedes and set the security system before entering the cool, dark interior of Maxime's Impressionistic Hair. Beauty salons gave him the willies, so he'd opted to spend the morning filling Carmen's prescription for antibiotics and making a late lunch appointment for the four of them at a popular seafood restaurant on the coast. It would be a good place to practice the art of eating out, he reasoned, thinking about the numerous formal meals they all had to get through on the cruise ship.

When he'd left his new "family" in the care of Maxime's capable—he hoped—hands, he'd had no idea what to expect. He just knew they had to look better than the motley crew he'd picked up at the side of the road yesterday afternoon. Nothing on earth, however, could have prepared him for what he found.

For there, waiting patiently in the lobby with two people he supposed were Helga and Carmen, was Emily.

And she was gorgeous.

Drop-dead, traffic-stopping, steal-your-breath-away gorgeous. He was positive she could walk into any modeling agency in the country and land a job. Yes, his heart pounded in his chest triumphantly, Roxanne would *hate* her.

Her chic new hairdo gave her a level of sophistication that most women strived for, but just missed, all their lives. Short, but not too short, its soft highlights glowed golden, a wispy frame for her cover-girl-quality face. Thick, dark eyelashes now surrounded her expressive brown eyes, and her alabaster complexion was offset only by her full, sensuous, plum-colored lips.

Ty felt his blood surge suddenly hot as he stared at her, and remembered the way she'd felt in his arms yesterday during their impromptu wrestling match.

"Hi," he breathed, feeling suddenly shy in the presence of this incredibly classy woman. "You look...you're..." Ty hadn't felt this awkward around a female since high school. "Beautiful."

"Thank you," she murmured as her eyes darted away from his, embarrassed by his close scrutiny.

"Didn't I tell you?" Max sashayed up to greet Ty and bask in the glory of his success. "Is she stunning or what?" Then he pointed at Carmen. "Come on, honey. Show Daddy your bow."

Giggling, Carmen spun around to show off her freshly trimmed and washed, midnight black French braid, tied with a large, red velvet bow.

She didn't look like the same kid at all, Ty marveled, shaking his head and smiling at her tiny, joy-filled face.

Then Max grabbed Ty by the arm and spun him to face Helga. "And, will you just look at Mama here?" He waved an airy hand in the older woman's direction.

Ty didn't think his poor heart could take any more shock as he gaped at what must have at one time been "the plastic lady."

Her salt-and-pepper hair curled in an attractive halo around her lightly made-up face, giving a softness to the features that had lived far too many hard years. Helga now looked every inch the standard-issue mother-in-law.

"Helga, you look fabulous," he said sincerely, causing her to blush a furious shade of red.

"Yeah, yeah, yeah," she muttered. "Save it."

Without raising an eyebrow, Ty signed the credit-card receipt and thanked Max profusely for a job well done. As he held the door open for his new-and-improved family, Helga paused and called out to one of Max's wizards.

"'Bye, Ralph, honey. You crack me up."

Barely acknowledging her departure, Ralph blew a stream of cigarette smoke at the ceiling and lazily winked in her direction.

"Uh, do you have to wear *that?*" Ty tugged at his collar. Why couldn't the old broad ever do anything normally? He glanced over at Emily for assistance.

Emily could only shrug helplessly.

"I don't see why not," Helga groused. "This outfit you just bought me cost a bloody fortune. This will keep it like new," she said, fluffing the large plastic shampoo cape Ralph had given her as a souvenir of her trip to Maxime's.

"Yes, that's true." Ty spoke as politely as he could through his clenched teeth. "But this is a nice restaurant. Not a beauty salon."

"What's the difference?"

Ty threw up his hands in exasperation. Let her wear the damn thing. What did he care? He was far too exhausted after a day of chasing three fickle females around a shopping mall with his credit cards to argue. The only bright spot in his entire day had been watching Emily try on swimsuits.

His entire body tingled just thinking about it. She was about the sexiest thing he'd ever laid eyes on. If she'd asked, he would gladly have bought her every suit in the store, just to see her try them on. But she'd seemed content with two simple suits that had fit her enticing figure like a glove.

Suddenly realizing where he was, he shook his head slightly to clear the provocative image and darted a glance at Emily. She looked amazingly natural playing the part of the society wife, sitting there, helping Carmen off with her new summer coat.

Sophisticated, poised, and completely in control of the situation. More than he could say for himself, he mused, looking out the restaurant's huge plate-glass window at the panoramic view of the Pacific Ocean.

He'd have to watch the direction of his thoughts, he chided himself. Otherwise he'd end up the same kind of lust-crazed employer that Roxanne had turned out to be. Nah. He could never be that bad. His eyes slid over to Emily as she smiled her amazing smile at the child. Then again...

Ty was definitely letting the new-and-improved appearance of these three cloud his vision. They were not poised, sophisticated or in control, he thought, wincing as Helga began picking at her teeth with a salad fork. No. They were vagabonds. Wayfarers. Wanderers. He had to keep in mind that they had probably never even seen a salad fork before, let alone used one to eat a salad.

He couldn't let Emily's stunning good looks fool him into believing that they were anywhere near ready for Roxanne.

They had work to do. And plenty of it. That's why he'd brought them here today—to practice. And there was no time like the present to begin practicing.

Clearing his throat, Ty addressed his three new family members. "Now then," he began, feeling like Rex Harrison in *My Fair Lady*. Perhaps they should start with a round of elocution lessons? *The rain in Spain...* Glancing at Carmen, he changed his mind. Nah. Napkins. That's where they should start.

Pulling his napkin off his plate, he proceeded to demonstrate how it was used in a formal situation. "The first thing you always do, after you sit down at a table, is take the napkin off the plate or wherever and put it in your lap, like this." Feeling like an idiot, he demonstrated as the three women in his life stared at him as though he were speaking Greek. He didn't care. They had to know this stuff if they were going to fool Roxanne.

Smiling slightly, Emily copied his maneuvers with the napkin, and awkwardly helped Carmen do the same. Helga yanked her napkin off the plate, flapped it open, and stuffed it under her chin.

Ty rolled his eyes and gave up. Maybe they should practice at home, where he could swear out loud.

"Ty?" a deep male voice asked as its owner approached their table. "Tyler Newroth? Is that you?"

Ty pulled his head up out of his hands just in time to see Denny Delmonico arrive at their table. Uncle Denny. Roxanne's Uncle Denny. Owner-of-Connstarr Uncle Denny. *Damn.*

"Mr. Delmonico! Good to see you, sir." Smiling, Ty scrambled to stand and grasp the proffered hand.

The short, plump, balding man pumped Ty's hand enthusiastically as his twinkling eyes swept the table. "The pleasure is all mine, son. And please, call me Denny," he instructed in his loud, jolly voice. "This must be your lovely wife. Roxanne told me you were recently married." He reached over and clasped Emily's hand in a warm greeting.

"Looks like she'll have no trouble keeping you in line," he exclaimed jovially, referring to the bruise under his eye.

"Yes, sir." Ty shot a bemused look at the red-faced Emily.

"You are a lucky son of a gun, Ty, old boy," Uncle Denny said, his eyes straying to Helga. "Hoarding three such beautiful women all to yourself should be a crime!"

Quickly snatching off her hairdresser's cape and tossing it onto the floor, Helga preened under the male attention and held her hand out to Uncle Denny, who took it and pressed it to his lips.

Tyler was too stunned to remember his manners. His heart was racing a mile a second. *They weren't ready! They hadn't rehearsed!* What the hell was he going to do now? Uncle Denny was actually kissing this loose cannon's hand. Good Lord, he thought, clutching at his collar and gasping for air, he was having a stroke.

"And you are?" Uncle Denny seemed not to notice Ty's discomfiture or lack of manners as he gazed into Helga's mischievous eyes.

"His mom," she said, and grinned devilishly at Ty.

Ty blanched.

"Sweetheart, are you all right?" Emily asked, wifely concern written all over her carefully made-up face. "You seem a little pale." She reached out to grasp Ty's arm as he sank back down into his seat.

"Fine, honey, just fine," he muttered.

Denny frowned at Ty. "You haven't been working too hard, have you son?" Turning his attention back to Helga, he said, "You must be real proud of your boy."

"Well, I like to think he wouldn't be where he is today without me." Helga winked flirtatiously up at Denny. "We haven't ordered yet, Denny, old boy, so why don't you sit on down with us and take a load off?"

Much to Ty's chagrin, Uncle Denny didn't need to be asked twice.

"Why—" he chuckled at Helga's delightful turn of phrase "—don't mind if I do."

For Ty, the entire meal passed in a haze. Luckily for him, Denny kept the conversational ball rolling with Helga and Carmen, while Emily cast an occasional worried glance in his direction. He still couldn't believe what was happening.

Helga's ribald laughter and bawdy jokes would have been the death of him, if Denny hadn't seemed completely charmed by her incredible lack of social grace. Thank heaven for Emily.

For even though Denny managed to put her on the spot more than once, she fielded his questions with an inborn sense of grace. If her answers were less than logical, well, that wasn't her fault. Maybe, sometime between now and Monday night, he could get her alone and they could work on getting their "marriage" story straight. His eyes strayed back to Emily, who was looking suddenly flustered.

"I don't know... I guess that would be all right," she hedged.

Emily's uncertain voice snapped Tyler out of his reverie and back into the conversation at hand. What were they talking about? He shrugged helplessly at her, looking for clues to the topic.

Seeming to take his body language as noncommittal, Emily made an executive decision.

"I know Carmen would be thrilled. And I'm sure if... Mother Helga would like to attend, we'd all love to. Wouldn't we, hon?"

What? Love to what? Tyler's panic-stricken eyes were practically boring her in two with their intensity, as he tried to figure out what Mother Helga and Carmen would love to do with Uncle Denny. He smiled bravely and tried to exude that good, old Connstarr corporate confidence.

"Ah, I guess so." Whatever. If it made the owner of the company happy, then sure, hell, he'd go along with it.

"That's great!" Uncle Denny beamed, joyfully pounding the table till the china rattled. "I just know you'll have a great time."

Helga snorted with glee. "Are you kidding, Denny, old boy? I'll have you know, I bleed Dodger blue!" Yanking her napkin from around her throat, she wiped at the glob of salad dressing on her chin.

"You're a Dodgers fan?" Uncle Denny's eyes misted slightly. "My dear, I had a feeling you were a woman after my own heart."

Punching the red-faced Denny affectionately in the arm, Helga said, "Fan? I practically lived at that stadium. Well, actually, I lived under the blea—"

Tyler tossed his wineglass into the middle of the table in an effort to shut Helga up. "Oh, I'm so sorry! How clumsy of me," he apologized, and shot Emily a glance that could wither the centerpiece on the table. Now not only was Emily going to the first big client meeting in his new position this coming Monday, but Helga and Carmen, too? They would never be able to pull this escapade off in front of Roxanne. Let alone a savvy client.

"You knucklehead," Helga huffed, and tossed her napkin over the river of wine that channeled its way across the table. "He always was a clumsy child," she said, assuming the role of martyred mother with gusto.

Emily smiled sympathetically at Ty. "Cheer up, hon. It could happen to anyone."

No. Not anyone. Just him. This could only happen to him.

Emily giggled. "You have to admit, it was pretty funny when your mother tried to show Uncle Denny her tattoo."

Ty groaned. "She's *not* my mother. *My* mother would roll over in her grave if she were dead. We were never rich, but we were proud."

Studying Ty from where she sat across from him on the living room couch, she realized just how little she still knew about this mysterious man. He was an enigma. With his dark, brooding good looks and his snapping emerald eyes, it was hard to tell what he was thinking. Emily had a feeling that he was the type whose trust was hard-won. Something about the combination of cool aloofness he displayed in public and his desperate need for her help fascinated Emily. She'd never met anyone like him.

"Stop laughing," he groused. "Why couldn't she have said she was *your* mother?" Exhaling noisily, he walked over to the wet bar to get them each a couple of soft drinks.

"Because she likes you."

"Ha." Ty muttered a few unsavory opinions under his breath. "She likes to see me sweat." Crossing the room, he handed her a can of soda, and flopped tiredly on the couch across from her.

Helga and Carmen, exhausted from their big day of shopping and dining out, had turned in early, leaving Emily and Ty to spend the evening alone together. Sharing sandwiches in the living room had been Ty's idea, and that suited Emily fine. She was still full from their late-afternoon lunch with Uncle Denny.

"I think you handled the situation very well," she complimented in an effort to relieve some of the lines in his haggard expression.

"Mmm-hmm. Sure. If you call arguing with my mother about finishing all the food on my plate 'very well,' then I guess I did a swell job." Ty shook his head in disgust.

"She was just getting into her role. She really wants to help Carmen. And in some weird way, I think she wants to help you." Emily frowned thoughtfully. "Plus, you have to remember, it drives her crazy to see people throw away perfectly good food."

"Is that why she plowed through the leftovers on Uncle Denny's plate?"

"He didn't seem to mind." Emily laughed. "I think he's taken with her."

"I think he's taken leave of his senses."

"Just be thankful she didn't lick her plate clean. She taught Carmen that charming habit."

"Oh, good grief."

Emily smiled at the pained expression on his face. "Come on, Ty. Admit it. She did just fine. Especially considering we weren't expecting to meet anyone from your company for at least another week."

"Yeah." Ty nodded grudgingly. "When she wasn't sending me into cardiac arrest, I guess she was fine." Propping his arms on his knees, he reached for a sandwich and took a healthy bite. After a moment he swallowed and said, "We have a lot of work to do this next week. All of us. But, most especially, you and me."

"Us? Why?"

"Because we're the married ones. High school sweethearts and all that. We have to know everything about each other, or Roxanne will eat us for breakfast." Taking a swig of his drink, a pensive expression crossed his face. "I think we should all rehearse the family thing on the weekends, mornings and early evenings. Then, after Mom and the kid hit the rack, you and I will stay up and practice our thing."

Emily felt a surge of dread mixed with anticipation snake its way between her shoulder blades and slither down her spine. Just what did he mean when he said "practice our thing"? Dying of curiosity, but afraid to ask, she nodded and managed to ask, "Oh?"

"Sure," Ty mumbled around bites of his sandwich. "You know, we should make up some stuff about our past and call each other honey and sweetheart and, you know, hold hands and whatever it is that newlyweds do." He awkwardly averted his eyes from hers for a moment. "Not that you need that much work. I mean, you were really great in the restaurant today. I think Uncle Denny was impressed."

Picking up her sandwich, Emily took a large bite so that she wouldn't have to respond to what he'd just said. Her heart tapped a sporadic rhythm in her breast as she tried valiantly to swallow what must have been a delicious sandwich, although it tasted like cardboard to her. What exactly was it that newlyweds did? What did he think they did? Just how much practice did they need? Her gaze strayed to his masculine, chiseled lips, and her stomach tightened with nervous expectation.

In an effort to rein in her emotions, she forced her thoughts to her research. She had to stay on target, she told herself sternly. The plight of the homeless was her main concern here.

"So, what do you think? I think we should start now. The sooner we get into character, the better chance we have of getting Roxanne off my back."

"Uh, sure." Emily tried to swallow the last cardboard bite. "Um...well...where should we begin?"

"Well, *honey.*" He grinned easily at her. "I'll go get my high school yearbook, and fill you in on some of the pertinent background info."

"Okay, uh, *honey.*" How awkward that one little word felt, when Uncle Denny wasn't around to impress. She felt the heat steal up her neck to her cheeks.

As Ty left the room to hunt up his annual, Emily tried to remember again why she'd agreed to this ridiculous charade, and how it related to what she was in L.A. for in the first place. It was then she remembered the pleasure on Carmen's face when Ty had bought her the baby doll with the eyes that blink, today at the mall. Yes. It was worth it. Every wacky hoop she had to jump through. For that one moment alone, it was worth it.

"Oh, *honey.* You're kidding!" Emily cried, pointing to the photo of Tyler as a junior varsity football player, whose soulful dark eyes stared at her from the depths of his gaunt little face. "That's you?"

Tyler smiled nostalgically. "That's me, all right, honey. All fifty pounds."

It was well after midnight, and they were both sprawled out on the living room floor, studying the array of photo albums and yearbooks spread out around them. At first the endearments had seemed very stilted to Emily as she'd struggled to refer to her latest employer as honey and sweetheart. But the more they practiced, the easier it became, until soon it almost seemed second nature.

"You were so cute, darling," she gushed, affecting adoration.

Tyler howled with laughter. "You're good. I can almost believe you think the scarecrow in that picture is cute!" Reaching out, he affectionately ruffled her new, short hairdo.

"Well, he is!" Emily batted her eyes coquettishly at him. "My little cutie pie." Speaking baby talk, she patted the picture with wifely affection.

"Ha! Knock it off, sweetheart. You're embarrassing me." Ty ducked his head under his arm, pretending to be shy as his body shook with laughter.

His carefree mood was contagious.

"Oh, now, *honey*... There's no need to be shy!" Emily tried to pry his arm off his head. "It's just me, the little woman. The one who knows *all* your secrets," she teased, giggling as Ty buried his head farther under his arm. Reaching down along his rib cage, she prodded his ribs with her fingertips, till he had to come up for air.

He tried to feign petulance over his laughter as he slapped the photo album closed and dragged it under his belly. "I'm not gonna show you any more pictures, if you're gonna laugh at me, *honey!*" He pouted.

"Who's laughing?" She giggled, and dived for the photo album.

"Yeah, right," he panted, pulling her hands out from under him and pinning her down on the floor beside him. "I'd like to see a picture of you when you hit adolescence."

Emily rolled her eyes. "I was a fairy princess, honey. You know that," she gasped, trying to wrest her arms from his firm grasp and abscond with the book, still hidden under his strong body.

Laughing, Ty reached under his belly and sent the album sailing across the living room floor as she attempted to tickle and burrow her way into the pictures of his past.

"Oh, no, you don't, Cinderella," he grunted. Grabbing her arms, he held them over her head with one hand, and plunged the other into her soft, silky hair. "It's not fair," he complained, his face only inches from hers. "You know everything about me, and I don't know anything about you. Maybe..." His breathing became somewhat ragged. "Maybe you are some kind of character out of a fairy tale. Is that it? Are you here to grant me a wish?" His eyes grew dark as they roamed her face, trying to discover what they could about her silent past.

Emily knew that the nature of their friendly wrestling match had taken a sudden, serious turn, and she stilled as he hovered above her, her heart palpitating irregularly. She wished she could read his mind as his fathomless gaze raked over her with an intensity that left her feeling somehow scalded.

"Because if that's the case, I wish..." He lowered his mouth slightly at an angle over hers. "I wish..." he whispered, his lips brushing hers lightly. "I..." His words were lost as his mouth found hers.

She wanted to fight it. She wanted to deny that his soft, sweet, electrifying kiss had any effect at all on her analytical, research-oriented mind. She wanted to remain cool, detached, uninvolved in this phase of her study. But, try as she might, she couldn't.

An involuntary moan, whispered soft in her throat, must have answered any doubts Ty might have had, because he released her arms from where he'd captured them over her head and, pulling her closer still, deepened the kiss.

She marveled at the almost unbearably exquisite sensations he evoked as his mouth explored hers. Drawing her fingers up to where their lips met, she traced the stubble up along his jaw and into his thick, brown hair, exploring its texture like a woman starved. It wasn't until that moment that Emily realized she'd been homeless all her life. Drifting. Incomplete. Because the moment Tyler's mouth settled over hers, Emily knew she had come home. For the first time in her life. And even though she felt a passion—dangerously close to flaring out of control—lurking beneath the gentle touch of his mouth, she believed with all her heart, at that moment, that she'd found safe harbor with Ty.

"Emily!" The tiny voice barely penetrated her foggy mind. "Emily. ¿Donde está?" Carmen's tearful voice reached her from the top of the stairs.

Reluctantly, and with obvious frustration, Ty pulled his mouth from hers and allowed her to sit up.

"Just a minute, sweetheart," she called to the frightened child. "I'll be right there. Okay?"

"Okay," the young girl sniffed as her pajama-clad feet scuffed across the hardwood floor toward her room.

Flustered, Emily glanced at Ty, and straightened the new clothes he'd bought her that afternoon. "She has a problem with nightmares, so I should go."

"Of course." Standing, Ty held his hand out and pulled her to her feet. He looked suddenly boyish and vulnerable, his eyes darting uncertainly to the floor and then back to hers. "Thanks for practicing the newlywed thing with me tonight," he said offhandedly, as though the intimate moment they had just shared was all part of the act. "I think it went pretty well, for... you know, our first try."

Obviously the moment had far more of an impact on her than it had on him, Emily reflected, feeling foolish at having gotten so carried away with the part she was playing. "Sure. No problem. Tomorrow we'll practice the family thing."

"Right. I have the day planned out for tomorrow," he told her, suddenly all-business. "If you, and the two of them, could be downstairs and in casual clothes by 8:00 a.m., that would be perfect."

"Eight it is." She nodded, imitating his demeanor. "Well, then—" she turned to leave the living room, flustered by his sudden change in temperature "—good night."

"Good night," he echoed. As she started up the stairs he corrected himself. "I mean, good night, honey."

Glancing down at him, she saw him grin as he headed back toward the living room.

Saturday, July 23.
Dear Diary:
Today I was able to observe Helga and Carmen as they were integrated into society. I was truly amazed at how well they both did, all things considered. Perhaps this could be another angle to contemplate for my thesis? Integrating the homeless. Hmm. I'll have to give it a lot of thought.

I, on the other hand, am not faring as well as my two compatriots. My main problem seems to be remembering why I'm here. I need to refocus, regroup, get back on track.

Tomorrow is a new day. After a good night's sleep, I'm sure I'll be able to concentrate, without distraction, on my project.

Chapter Five

Ty stripped off his shirt and crossed his bedroom floor to open the French doors that led to his veranda. Running the wadded-up shirt lightly over his body, he could feel the warm coastal breeze begin to cool his overheated flesh. What on earth had possessed him to kiss her? he berated himself, and dropped into a white cast-iron chair near the railing. That certainly hadn't been part of his "rehearsal" schedule.

Rolling around on his living room floor with a homeless woman he'd picked up at the side of the road was not his usual style for Saturday night. No. Usually he could be found at one of Boston's finer restaurants, in the company of a beautiful and exciting socialite.

Why, then, was his heart still racing at the thought of holding Emily in his arms? He didn't even know her last name, and yet he somehow felt closer to her than he ever had with Boston's most elite, even after months of dating. Lightly scratching his chest, he hoped there'd been no harm done. He'd wanted her to get used to being a newlywed, hadn't he? Maybe they shouldn't practice kissing unless someone else was around, though. No telling where another one of those stupefying kisses could lead.

He stared, unseeing, down at the glassy surface of his pool. There must be something about California that brought out the stupidity in him. Since moving here, he'd done nothing but make one dumb decision after another. What ever happened to the hard-driving, workaholic businessman with the neon future? Ha. He'd traded that glory in on the chance to be husband, father, henpecked son and harassed employee to three wild women and a heretic. It seemed his brilliant career at Connstarr was crumbling before his very eyes. And there wasn't a damn thing he could do about it. Not with Roxanne as ringmaster of this circus.

Ty sighed in futility and propped his bare feet on the veranda railing. This was never going to work. How could they ever hope to pull it off? he wondered dismally, leaning back on the hind legs of his chair and staring up at the star-filled sky.

Even if Roxanne were to buy their story, how long would that last? Helga would undoubtedly build some kind of plastic monstrosity on the poop deck of the ocean liner, or Carmen would suddenly spill the homeless beans to some bilingual member of the Connstarr management team.

Groaning, he let his head fall back against the back of his chair. His life was a complete and total mess. And what did Tyler Newroth do after a wild weekend of screwing up his life?

"I'm going to Disneyland," he muttered. Standing tiredly, he dragged himself to bed.

"Pepperoni or Canadian bacon and pineapple?" Ty held the pizza box up for Emily's inspection. It was late the following evening and they were sitting alone in the cabana by the side of his pool. Two tapered candles stuffed into empty soda cans glowed cheerfully in the dark, casting a romantic glow across the table.

"Nothing for me." She sighed contentedly and tossed her napkin onto her paper plate.

"Oh, come on," he chided. "I had to slave over a hot phone for this meal. Besides, after what happened today, you need your strength."

Emily blushed. "I'm feeling much better now, thank you," she replied somewhat churlishly, and wriggled with embarrassment in her seat. How would she ever live down the humiliation of getting seasick on Mark Twain's stern-wheeler at Disneyland that morning? How mortifying to be the most interesting spectacle on the ride.

Ty had been wonderful, though. So patient and under-standing, as she leaned over the rail and fed the fish. He'd held her head and patted her back, while murmuring soothing words in her ear. Helga, the human megaphone, on the other hand, had loudly ordered the crowd to give her room.

"Get back!" she'd shouted, pushing and shoving any-one who dared get too close to her precious Emily. "You don't want to get any on you, do you?" she'd hollered at the curious onlookers.

Emily could have cheerfully thrown herself overboard. She was sure this ignominious experience would end up gracing more than one family photo album.

She smiled ruefully across the table at Ty.

"Come on. Just one more piece," he cajoled, flipping a slice of pepperoni across the table at her plate. "You're too skinny as it is."

"I am not," she protested hotly, and lifting the pizza to her mouth, tore off a huge bite. Skinny, indeed! She may not be as voluptuous as old Roxanne was reported to be, but she had a few curves here and there.

"Okay," he conceded. "Not skinny, exactly. But an ex-tra slice of pizza won't kill you. You ate like a bird all day."

"That's because I didn't want a repeat performance of the boat ride once we got on the Matterhorn," she groused. "Helga probably would have strapped me to her back and rappelled down the mountain, screaming bloody murder for a medic."

"That's my mom." Ty chuckled and grabbed a slice of Canadian-bacon pizza out of the box he'd ordered after Helga and Carmen had gone to bed. "It's amazing how sensitive you are to seasickness," Ty marveled, and shook his head. "That river ride today barely moved."

Emily winced. If he only knew just how terrified she was of being out on the water in a boat. She still had no idea how she was going to make it through this cruise of his. Taking a deep breath, she stiffened her resolve and knew that if it would help Helga and Carmen, she would cross the ocean in a canoe.

Ty thoughtfully chewed his pizza. "At least this way we know you are prone to seasickness and we can get some of those patches for you. We can't have you spend the entire cruise hanging over the edge of the rail. Actually, it's kind of fortunate it happened the way it did today."

"Fortunate? You call having my mother-in-law shouting 'She's gonna blow!' fortunate?" Emily bristled indignantly. "I have never been so humiliated in my life."

Ty regarded her curiously as he poured them both another glass of wine. "Getting seasick today was one of the worst things that has ever happened to you?" Lifting his glass to his lips, he watched her over the rim.

"Yes. No. Well, you know what I mean," she hedged, not wanting to explore this path any further. It wouldn't do to have him thinking she was some kind of hothouse flower. She was a tough street person, she reminded herself. Getting sick on a ride at Disneyland was nothing compared to life on the streets. "I don't know what got into me." She shrugged, trying to lead him away from the fact that she was such a wimp when it came to boats. "Must have been a bad frozen banana."

The corner of Ty's mouth quirked and he nodded slowly. "Must have been. But, just to be on the safe side, we'll get you something for seasickness before we go."

Secretly relieved, Emily tried to appear nonchalant and shrugged again. Thank heavens. She couldn't very well tell Ty that she always got seasick. Most homeless people she knew didn't have much opportunity to go boating. She could just see Helga chasing the Connstarr bigwigs away while Emily tossed her own version of confetti over the rail of the ocean liner. She guessed he was right. It was a good thing he'd found out about her problem now.

Besides, it really hadn't interfered with the fun today at all. Carmen had been completely enthralled by the happiest place on earth, and even Helga had seemed enchanted by the Magic Kingdom.

"It was awfully nice of you to take Carmen on the Small World ride so many times. That was above and beyond the call of duty," Emily said appreciatively, and peeked through the candlelight at the man seated across from her. He stretched his arms up over his head, and she admired the way the muscles in his chest flexed and moved beneath his shirt. She wondered if he had any idea at all just how attractive he was. With his beautiful, dark brown hair, and his chiseled movie-star looks, it was no wonder his boss was after him.

"Oh, no big deal. I only lost half my mind. Besides, it was worth it to see the look of rapture on her little face." He grinned and dropped to his elbows on the table. "She's a doll. I can see why you and Helga are so protective of her."

Nodding, Emily took a small sip of her wine. "Helga tells me that this last year has been pretty rough on her." She ran her fingers slowly over the rim of her glass. "As soon as I'm finished with my job for you, I want to see about getting her placed with a family through an adoption service. I know there must be some family out there that would just love her to pieces."

A paternal look of concern momentarily crossed Ty's handsome face. "But how could you be sure? How do you know that the new family would love her as much as you do? Or worse, what if no one wanted her at all?"

Emily shook her head ruefully. "I wouldn't know. But, I'm beginning to think being passed around by the system has to be better than being out on the street."

The muscles in his jaw worked angrily, and Emily could see that Carmen's situation was starting to affect him the same way it affected her. It was hard to believe that life wasn't all sunshine and rainbows for such a small child. And, unfortunately, it wasn't just the one small child. There were literally thousands of children out there who weren't even as well-off as Carmen was.

"Hey," she admonished, trying to lighten his mood. "You're taking good care of her now, and that's something. And today you gave her an adventure she will probably never forget."

"Doesn't seem like a whole hell of a lot." He shook his head in disgust. "It's so easy to take things for granted. A warm bed. A hot meal. And then you meet a kid like Carmen and it kind of knocks you for a loop."

She knew exactly how he felt. "Mmm-hmm."

"She kind of worms her way into your heart, doesn't she?"

Emily smiled sadly. "In a big way."

He glanced at her, then focused on the candle flame. "I was pretty freaked when she disappeared after the teacup ride," he admitted, referring to the few tortured minutes that Carmen had gotten turned around and lost in the crowd. "And then when I found her standing there crying, holding on to Mickey's giant hand, it almost broke my heart."

Sensing that this type of admission did not come easily to a man like Ty, Emily just sat and listened.

He pushed his chair slightly away from the table and crossed an ankle over his knee. "You know, when she saw me and smiled that big, watery-eyed smile, I thought I'd bust." He ran a weary hand over his face, and around to the back of his neck. "I got lost at Coney Island when I was a little boy," he reflected. "It was pretty scary. I hated that she had to go through that."

"I know," Emily murmured. "And the sad part is, in her short life, she's been through so much worse."

"So have you."

Emily could tell that he was dying of curiosity about her past. And she was dying to tell him. But she couldn't. Not yet.

"It hasn't been nearly as bad for me," she replied, leading him away from thin conversational ice. "It's a lot harder on the children."

The poignant moment gripped them both, and they sat, filled with a heavy sense of melancholy, regarding each other silently in the dancing glow of the candles. Shrouded in the intimate circle of light, they shared a moment together that slowly began to change the way they viewed one another.

"I learned a long time ago, you can't save them all," Emily murmured, twirling the stem of her glass between her thumb and fingers. "It was one of the most bitter pills I've ever had to swallow. But I know that if I can help just one or two people at a time, I'm moving forward."

Ty's curious green eyes were filled with admiration for her. "I've never spent much time worrying about anybody but myself," he admitted, his smile self-deprecating. "Unless you count people like Roxanne—people who get in my way."

"That's not true, Ty." Emily's voice was soft. "You're helping us. More than you'll ever know." Every time she thought about the creeps who could have picked her up at the side of the road, she was grateful all over again for his generosity.

"I'm glad I can help," he said sincerely, his eyes growing warm under her earnest praise. "Hey. Enough of this macabre conversation. It's too late to save the world today anyway. How about a quick dip before we turn in?"

Adrenaline surged through her veins. He might as well find out the truth now. Just another embarrassing thing he should probably be aware of before they set sail. "Uh ... actually, I don't swim," she admitted and, taking a deep breath, peered into the darkness through the flickering candles at him for his reaction.

"You don't swim?"

"No, but that's okay, I'll be happy to watch you. Go ahead," she suggested, hoping he'd back off.

"Oh, you should learn to swim. It could save your life someday. You could drown without the basics."

Emily grimaced. "No, really. I solve the whole problem by staying away from the water altogether." She smiled brightly.

"Come on. I insist." Ty waved a confident hand in her direction. "No big deal. I can teach you. We should probably practice being married some more anyway. After all, tomorrow night is our big debut with Roxanne."

A jolt of fear ran down her spine. So soon? Were they ready? Looking across the table at this powerful, confident businessman, Emily's fears somewhat dissipated. He must know what he's doing.

"Okay, uh, sure," she agreed as more than one doubt about this swimming lesson entered her mind. Hesitating, she stood to leave. "A swimming lesson sounds ... er, uh, okay, I guess. I'll just go get my suit," she promised, and headed into the house.

Learning to swim before the cruise was probably a good idea, she admitted grudgingly to herself. Especially since she was notorious for sinking like a rock. And, unfortunately, she was even worse in the water than on it. Her twin sister Erica must have hogged all the genes for water sports, for she adored swimming and boating. Too bad she wasn't here now, Emily mused as she trudged up the stairs to her room. Erica would probably prefer pinch hitting for her on a cruise to Mexico, to taking care of the less than delightful Spencer kids out in the middle of nowhere.

She should probably call Erica and check in, she reflected, rummaging through her drawer for her new bath-

ing suit. Find out how she was doing. Hopefully, she and
Will were getting along okay.

Will. Squeezing her eyes tightly shut, she tried to conjure
his image up in her mind, but visions of Ty's extraordinari-
ly handsome face interfered with her reception, and she finally gave up. The niggling worry that absence was definitely not making the heart grow fonder with Will bothered
her. Maybe she could talk it over with Erica, if she had a
chance to call her. But then again, maybe not. Erica would
only gloat, telling her that she always fell in love at the drop
of a hat, and then probably threaten to kill her for making
her stand in for her latest passing fancy. Poor Erica. Emily
winced as a pang of guilt assailed her. Hopefully someday
her twin would forgive her for making her spend her summer with the widower Will and his two holy terrors.

"Hey, hey, hey! Relax," Ty commanded, peeling Emily's arms from around his neck. She was coughing and
sputtering and—unfortunately for Ty—grabbing at anything solid she could get her terrified hands on, including his
nose, ears and hair. "You're okay," he soothed, pulling her
weightless, slippery body into his arms and up against the
solid wall of his chest.

Coughing, Emily clung to his neck and nodded, only letting go long enough to push her new, fashionably short
bangs out of her eyes.

"Okay?"

"Heh—hmm." She coughed.

"I guess this means we should hold off on the high-dive
lessons for a while," he joked as he slowly floated her over
to the pool's shallow end. "At least until we master dog
paddling." They'd been in the pool for more than an hour
and Emily was no closer to swimming than a concrete block.

"I'm sorry." She shook her hair out of her face and stared
at him with large, fearful brown eyes.

Drops of water glistened on her full, sensuous lips in the
moonlight, and Ty had to fight the overwhelming urge to

kiss her into oblivion. She probably wouldn't buy the rehearsal excuse this time. The reverberation of his heartbeat echoed in his head over the whine of the pool pump, and he knew that she was beginning to affect him a little more than he was comfortable with.

Squinting, she shifted to a position where she could more comfortably peer into his face. "I almost drowned once, when I was little," she admitted, reticent to reveal too much about her past. "And I haven't been very good around water ever since."

Ah-ha! So that's why she got seasick so easily and couldn't swim. She was afraid of drowning. "Understandable." Ty nodded. "But all the more reason for you to learn to swim. Here. Let's try floating again," he suggested, anxious to concentrate on something other than the amazingly smooth texture of her slick skin. Rearranging her across his chest, he slid his hands behind her back, and immediately she wound herself tightly around his body.

Ty smiled wryly down at her. As amazingly enjoyable as he found this to be, he knew that if she was ever going to float—and if he was going to hang on to the last vestiges of his control—she had to chill out.

"Sweetheart, relax," he pleaded, as though coaxing a frightened child. "I promise I won't let go. There is no way on earth you can drown. Honest. It's only three feet deep at this end."

"Th-th-three?"

"Three." He grinned. "Come on. Stand up." When she did, Ty put one hand on her smooth, bare midriff, and the other in the middle of her back. "Let's try floating on your back. I promise I won't drop you. Scout's honor." He held up three solemn fingers.

"Okay," she whispered tentatively, and pinched her nose tightly shut.

"Just relax," he instructed, wishing he could follow his own advice. He was strung more tightly than an electric guitar. That neon pink scrap of material she called a swimsuit was doing shameful things to his libido. "And try," he said, attempting to get her to loosen up a little, "not to pinch your nose off."

She stuck her tongue out at him as he swept her into his arms. Slowly, Ty lowered her body into the water, cradling her bottom on his bent knees and supporting her legs and head with his arms.

"There now." He smiled down at her. "This isn't so bad, is it?"

Quickly shaking her head, Emily concentrated on relaxing. "No... um, not bad, really. Just strange."

"Yeah, but that's true of everything until you get used to it. Here, let's go over to where the water is a little deeper."

She nodded up at him, her wide eyes never leaving his face.

"Now, look, you're nearly floating by yourself," he said proudly, trying not to notice the tiny patches of swimsuit bob and sway as they broke the surface of the water. Holy heart failure, he thought, willing his breathing to slow down. There was no way that Roxanne could ever compete with *this* at the side of the pool. Emily was perfect. Tightening his grip—to reassure her, he told himself—he led her farther into the deep end.

She beamed up at him, obviously proud that she hadn't panicked yet.

"All right, it's only four and a half feet deep here. You can still stand up if you want to, so remember to stay relaxed, and keep breathing deep, slow breaths." Sucking in a lungful of air, he demonstrated for her, his chest moving her up and down in the water as he breathed.

Pulling her head out of the water, she rolled her eyes expressively and tried to speak around the hand that still held her nose tightly shut. "I'mb not habing a baby here. Just don leb aby water geb in by bouth, so I can breab," she instructed him nasally.

She was so incredibly beautiful, even with her cheeks puffed out that way. How he'd love to skip the rest of this lesson and...

No. He couldn't do anything to blow her trust now. And not just because he needed her help with Roxanne.

"If you're ready, I'm going to let go of you. Whatever you do, stay calm. If you start to sink, I'll grab you, okay?"

"Okay."

"Okay." Ty took a deep breath, and slowly, ever so slowly, pulled his hands out from behind her back. "I'm only holding you with one hand," he informed her enthusiastically.

Eyes shining, she asked, "Really?"

"Really. We'll just stay like this for a second or two while you get used to floating."

"Okay." Her eyes still clung to his, as though they were some kind of lifeline that contained the supernatural power to elevate her.

When he felt that she was totally relaxed and ready, he made his move. "Here we go," he warned as he slowly removed his remaining hand from beneath her back.

She was floating. All by herself, she was floating. Ty experienced a surge of accomplishment he hadn't felt in years. A feeling that he had done something important. Even more important than acquiring new business for Connstarr.

"Hey, sweetheart," he whispered to her, his chest swelling with happiness. "You're floating. All by yourself. I'm not even touching you."

The happy smile on her face turned upside down. "You're not?" she asked worriedly.

"No!" he crowed. "You're on your own."

"I am?" she shrieked just before she sank like a pair of lead gangster shoes.

"You were." Ty sighed as he dived beneath the surface to fish her up out of the water. When he emerged, predictably, he was wearing a gasping and sputtering Emily, coiled firmly around his shoulders and chest.

"I'm sorry," she cried, burying her nose into his neck, disappointment filling her voice. "I must have panicked."

"Hey," he said as he gently pried her face out of the crook of his neck so that he could look at her. "You did it!"

"I did?" She sniffed, rubbing the water out of her eyes and probing his for the truth.

"Yes!" He threw back his head and yelled, jubilant over her first tentative victory. *"You did it!"*

"I did it?" she shouted, laughing with him and hugging him tightly around the neck.

Slipping his arms around her slender waist, he hugged her back, thrilled by their breakthrough. "You sure did." He pressed her snugly into his arms and squeezed, kissing the top of her head, her forehead, her eyes, her cheeks.

She stilled in his arms and looked slowly up at him, her eyes still shining with pleasure, and he became suddenly aware that she was cradled against his body with nothing but two, practically nonexistent, pink slivers of material separating them. And—much to his chagrin—he felt himself begin to react to her in a way that was purely physical.

His throat grew dry as he battled the tension that was coiling so tightly in his gut. The smell of the chlorine seemed intoxicating, and Tyler was sure she must be able to feel the chugging locomotive that was his heartbeat thudding against her breast. Swallowing hard, he knew that he should climb out of the pool now. Before it was too late. But it was already too late.

A tiny whimper of protest sounded from somewhere deep in her throat as he lowered his head and lightly brushed his lips over hers. But if she objected, she made no move to stop him, and—disgusted with himself for his own lack of control—he increased the pressure and kissed her deeply. Slowly at first and then, as he built steam, more savagely.

Backing her into the shallow end, he lifted her up onto the built-in steps, and leaned heavily against her, cradling her head against the edge of the pool. She tasted of water and wine, and the combination increased rather than quenched his thirst for her. As much as he wanted to, he couldn't seem to find the wherewithal to resist her, and as his mouth roughly plundered hers, he knew he was no better than Roxanne.

He'd always prided himself on his ability to remain objective with his co-workers. What was it about Emily, then, his latest employee, that allowed him to step over lines that he'd drawn years ago?

Stop! his conscience urged him, even as he tore his mouth from hers to continue his assault down along her jaw to her neck and from there to the place where the water met her breastbone.

Small, mewling sounds of pleasure coming from deep within her throat only served to fuel his craving—a craving so voracious it threatened to drown him. Kneeling on the steps, between her legs, he grasped her head in his hands, and pulled her mouth back to his. Her soft, full lips blended perfectly with his, and he lost all rational idea of where his body ended and hers began.

It was okay, he told himself, feeling her hands twining around his neck, pulling him closer into the soft arch of her body. This was all just part of the plan. If they were really going to fool Roxanne, this research they were doing would come in handy.

Bull! his conscience barked, louder this time. This was no experiment. She was beginning to get under his skin. Bigtime. And before he damaged their tentative trust any more than he probably already had, he knew he had to stop now, or lose everything. Steeling himself against her potent allure, he slowly pulled his mouth from hers.

Gasping raggedly with frustration, he shook his head as if to clear the murky mess he'd just made, and wondered, now that he'd had a taste of heaven, how could he ever stay away?

Fool.

His conscience was playing hardball tonight.

Before he could change his mind, he gripped her upper arms firmly in his hands and hauled her up out of the water and onto the concrete deck. Emily gazed up at him, confusion mixed with hurt mirrored in her foggy expression.

Averting his eyes, Ty knew that if he didn't look away, he'd haul her into the house and break every rule he'd ever made for himself, risking his career for a moment's pleasure. He couldn't let this happen. She was his employee, for crying out loud. His future at Connstarr rested on her willingness to help. And, homeless or not, he had the distinct feeling that this woman did not give her physical self lightly.

"I suppose we should probably call it a day," he said gruffly, attempting to keep her at arm's length, not trusting himself to be kind to her. The slightest bit of encouragement on her part and he would be lost. "I think that we're probably as ready as we'll ever be."

She stared up at him, mortification written all over her lovely face. He could have kicked himself around the block for being such a heartless jerk.

"Uh, yes. Ready as we'll ever be," she repeated hollowly. "Good night," she said curtly and, spinning on her heel, marched, shoulders square, into the house.

He stared after her, still suffering from a case of the bends, after forcing himself to surface so quickly from their kiss. Raking his hands over his face, he fell into the pool and let himself sink to the bottom. It was for the best, he decided, watching the tiny air bubbles that escaped from his mouth float toward the pool's shimmery light. He'd be damned if he was ever going to treat someone in his employ the way Roxanne treated him.

Pushing off the floor of the pool, he soared to the surface and gasped for air. What an idiot. If he knew what was good for him, he would arrange for a red-eye to Boston that night. This situation was getting crazier by the minute. Last week, he'd led a perfectly mundane life as a normal, hardworking businessman. This week, he was a fugitive from his lust-crazed boss, fighting a growing desire for a street person he'd found at the side of the road.

He dragged himself out of the water and ran a towel over his head. He couldn't even begin to imagine what new insanity lay ahead for him tomorrow.

"Women," he muttered, and headed into the house.

After peeling herself out of her wet swimsuit, Emily pulled the new lacy nightgown Ty had purchased for the cruise over her still-damp skin. Leaning into the bathroom sink, she splashed cold water on her face in an effort to still the inferno that raged in her cheeks.

What in heaven's name had prompted her to throw herself at her new boss that way? she wondered, shuddering at her wanton behavior in the pool. He obviously thought she was no better than the oversexed Roxanne. The look of disgust on his face as he'd sent her off to bed, like some kind of recalcitrant child, told her that.

Groaning, she stuck her whole head under the icy spray, and bit her lower lip in shame. When would she ever learn? Her sister was always accusing her of rushing headlong into what she fancied to be love.... And as much as Emily hated to admit it, her sister was always right.

But still, there was something decidedly different about her reaction to Tyler Newroth. She pulled her head out of the frigid water and ran a towel over her hair. Glancing up into the mirror, she could see where the stubble from his beard had turned her lips and cheeks a soft pink. Her heart did a full gainer with a half twist as she thought about their intimate swimming lesson.

This was ridiculous, she chided herself, and, tossing her damp towel over the shower door with her swimsuit, strode purposefully back to her room. She was acting like some kind of lovesick teenager. This nonsense had to stop now. She was here to do her thesis research, damn it, and that's what she intended to do. Tyler most certainly wasn't wasting any time sitting around thinking about the kiss he'd shared with the homeless woman, she was sure. He had bigger fish to fry. Well, by golly, so did she. Tomorrow she would prove to him that she could be as coolly serious about their bargain as he was.

Flopping across her bed, she grabbed her journal and flipped the pages to the day's entry. As she stared at the blank page, visions of Ty's handsome face danced across its surface, making it impossible for her to concentrate.

Finally, after much fruitless pondering, she scrawled one furious word and, slamming the book shut, pulled her pillow over her head.

Sunday, July 24.
Dear Diary:
Men!

SILHOUETTE®

AN IMPORTANT MESSAGE FROM THE EDITORS OF SILHOUETTE®

Dear Reader,

Because you've chosen to read one of our fine romance novels, we'd like to say "thank you"! And, as a **special** way to thank you, we've selected <u>four more</u> of the <u>books</u> you love so well, **and** a cuddly Teddy Bear to send you absolutely _**FREE!**_

Please enjoy them with our compliments...

Anne Canado

Senior Editor,
Silhouette Romance

P.S. And <u>because</u> we value our customers, we've attached something extra inside...

PEEL OFF SEAL AND PLACE INSIDE

HOW TO VALIDATE
YOUR
EDITOR'S FREE GIFT
"THANK YOU"

1. Peel off gift seal from front cover. Place it in space provided at right. This automatically entitles you to receive four free books and a cuddly Teddy Bear.

2. Send back this card and you'll get brand-new Silhouette Romance™ novels. These books have a cover price of $2.99 each, but they are yours to keep absolutely free.

3. There's no catch. You're under no obligation to buy anything. We charge nothing—ZERO—for your first shipment. And you don't have to make any minimum number of purchases—not even one!

4. The fact is thousands of readers enjoy receiving books by mail from the Silhouette Reader Service™ months before they're available in stores. They like the convenience of home delivery and they love our discount prices!

5. We hope that after receiving your free books you'll want to remain a subscriber. But the choice is yours—to continue or cancel, anytime at all! So why not take us up on our invitation, with no risk of any kind. You'll be glad you did!

6. Don't forget to detach your FREE BOOKMARK. And remember...just for validating your Editor's Free Gift Offer, we'll send you FIVE MORE gifts, *ABSOLUTELY FREE!*

GET A FREE
TEDDY BEAR . . .

You'll love this plush, cuddly Teddy Bear, an adorable accessory for your dressing table, bookcase or desk. Measuring 5½" tall, he's soft and brown and has a bright red ribbon around his neck — he's completely captivating! And he's yours *absolutely free*, when you accept this no-risk offer!

THE EDITOR'S "THANK YOU" FREE GIFTS INCLUDE:

▶ Four BRAND-NEW romance novels
▶ A cuddly Teddy Bear

DETACH AND MAIL CARD TODAY!

EDITOR'S
FREE
GIFT
SEAL
THANK YOU

YES! I have placed my Editor's "thank you" seal in the space provided above. Please send me 4 free books and a cuddly Teddy Bear. I understand I am under no obligation to purchase any books, as explained on the back and on the opposite page.

215 CIS ASV6 (U-SIL-R-05/95)

NAME

_____

ADDRESS   APT.

_____

CITY   STATE   ZIP

Thank you!

Chapter Six

"Play ball!"

The umpire's command reverberated throughout Dodger Stadium as Tyler led his "family" to Connstarr's special box seats. Thankfully, Roxanne, Uncle Denny and the potential client had yet to arrive. It would give him a chance to issue some last-minute instructions, Ty thought, herding the small group and their piles of peanuts, hot dogs and soft drinks to their seats.

The giant electronic scoreboard flashed the words Go Dodgers! as the organist whipped the crowd into a pregame frenzy. Helga, already caught up in the spirit of America's most beloved sport, dangerously swung her mustard-soaked hot dog and hollered, "Damn! How I love ya, Dodger Blue!"

Ty patted his jacket pocket to make sure he'd remembered his king-size bottle of antacids, and shot Emily a pointed look.

"Can't you do something to keep her under control?" he groaned under his breath as he guided her into the seat next to him.

"I left her muzzle at home," she flung back, pulling Carmen across her knees and settling her in her lap. "What do you want me to do?" Her tone was filled with exasperation. "Slip a Mickey Finn into her hot dog?"

"I don't care," Ty snapped. "Just try to keep her to a dull roar, okay?"

She'd been cool and aloof all day long, and Tyler was beginning to add her attitude to his long list of nightmares about this evening. She was no doubt huffy with him over that damn kiss they'd shared in the pool late last night. Okay. So it had been a stupid move on his part, but for now, anyway, they had to put it behind them and get on with the proceedings at hand. He didn't have time to baby-sit her emotions all evening long.

"What's with you, anyway?" he asked, irritated with her long-suffering expression. Maybe he should try to discuss and solve her problem before the other half of their party arrived.

"Nothing," she answered snippily as she fished a hot dog out of the small cardboard box and busied herself unwrapping it for Carmen.

Ty wanted to wring her delicate little neck. "Nothing?" he snorted, and, at Helga's insistent nudging, reached into Emily's carton and tossed the older woman another hot dog.

"Well," Emily said in a huffy whisper, "I don't know why *I* should have to be the one to keep her under control. After all, she is *your* mother." She turned and stared out at the playing field, unseeing.

"Oh, for crimeny sakes..." Ty exhaled noisily at the ceiling before turning sharply to face her. "Listen up," he commanded under his breath. "They will be here any second, and there are a few things I want to get straight with you right now."

Still gazing stubbornly out at the field, the muscles in Emily's throat worked as she tried to swallow past the nervous lump lodged there.

Firmly grasping her arm to gain her full attention, Ty continued. "First of all, if you will recall, it was *your* idea to invite the old battle-ax to join us tonight. And second, this could be one of the most important business meetings of my entire career." He pounded the armrest between their seats for emphasis, and Emily jumped. Her large brown eyes found and locked with his, and she sat, almost mesmerized as he continued.

"And, according to Roxanne, this client is a real family man, and the fact that I'm married to a loving woman could have a huge impact on the outcome of this deal." He tightened his grip convulsively on her arm. "I'm living up to my end of the bargain." Mentally he crossed his fingers behind his back. That kiss he'd given her last night wasn't exactly part of the deal, but he hoped she'd forget about that.

At the sound of Roxanne's shrill laughter echoing down the corridor into their box seats, Tyler stiffened. Taking a deep breath, he lowered his voice even further.

"And I expect you to live up to yours. So, *sweetheart*, start acting like a newlywed, because they're here." Gripping Emily firmly by the hand, he tried to control the flames that licked and danced in his belly. He stood and helped her with Carmen and the containers of food, so that she could rise to her feet while he made introductions.

On a cloud of heavy, cloying, and most likely very expensive perfume, Roxanne sashayed into the room. Uncle Denny's voice floated toward them from somewhere down the hallway as he led their guest to the box seats.

Roxanne's eyes, like two, beady, black, heat-seeking missiles, searched out and landed on Emily. Rudely raking her up and down, Ty could imagine her mentally calculating the cost of Emily's clothing, the stylist of her hair, the brands of her cosmetics, the depth and scope of her relationship with Tyler.

Tyler felt Emily straighten under Roxanne's merciless scrutiny and move imperceptibly closer to him. This was it. The moment they had worked toward all weekend long. The spotlight had kicked on and it was time for Emily to solo.

"Roxanne." Ty's carefully modulated voice belied none of the volcanic activity churning in his gut. "I'd like you to meet my wife, Emily Newroth. Emily, this is my boss, Roxanne Delmonico."

Leaning across Tyler, Emily extended a cordial hand. "Roxanne. At last we meet. I've heard so many... things about you."

Roxanne lifted a cool eyebrow as she limply took the proffered hand. "All marvelous, of course?"

"Of course."

Smiling blithely, Ty released his grip on Emily's arm with a reassuring squeeze. He hoped she would be all right alone with Roxanne for a moment, and with a quick wink, headed to the door to find Uncle Denny and the potential client.

Roxanne reluctantly tore her eyes from her perusal of what she considered to be her arch rival, and examined the small child peeking out at her from behind Emily's skirt.

"Well, now, who have we here?" she asked in her husky voice, her bright red lips stretching insincerely upward to reveal her expensive dental work.

Something about the way Roxanne's eyes narrowed at Carmen reminded Emily of the way that wicked witch in *The Wizard of Oz* eyeballed Toto.

Instinctively she wrapped her arms around the small child's shoulders and pulled her around front to stand tightly against her body.

"This is our daughter, Carmen. Say hello, sweetheart." Emily nudged Carmen.

"*¡Hola!*" Carmen grinned disarmingly up at the stunned Roxanne.

Tenting her fingers at her chin, Roxanne cocked her head quizzically as she studied the young girl. "Ah... From a previous marriage, I assume?"

"No," Emily automatically answered, going with the story she and Tyler had concocted. "I, uh, spent some time in Mexico...after high school," she said, "and became friends with Carmen's family. When they were tragically killed, I agreed to take Carmen in. And Tyler has been so sweet about the whole thing, agreeing to adopt her and all."

Roxanne gave her a glazed look and it was suddenly crystal clear to Emily why Ty was in such a jam with this woman. There was definitely something wrong with her. Something elemental missing in her personality. Emily couldn't quite put her finger on it, but her instincts warned her to beware.

"Isn't that sweet?" Roxanne gushed. "And how fortunate that we will be spending the next week in Mexico. Why, you—" she eyed Emily triumphantly "—can translate for us!" she cried, looking down her nose at Tyler's little family, clearly pitying the poor fool.

"Translate?" Emily licked her dry lips. She'd only had two years of high school Spanish. At best, she could compliment someone on a beautiful taco. How the heck was she supposed to learn Spanish before next Monday? For this kind of work, Tyler had better start making plans to build a college trust fund for Carmen, she fumed.

"Yes. You know," Roxanne purred, training her hawk-like gaze back on Emily, "show us how to barter with the locals, tell us where the nightlife is hot."

Emily knew of some caves in Mexico that would be perfect. Roxanne could hang upside down and enjoy the nightlife to her puny little heart's content. Her condescending attitude was rapidly getting on Emily's nerves.

"Ah, sí, no problema," she responded, racking her limited vocabulary for the proper words.

Thankfully, Tyler, followed by Uncle Denny and their guest, entered the seating area, saving Emily from any further bilingual tongue twisting. As her husband strode into the room, leading the owner of the company and his guest, Emily was suddenly aware of the raw power Ty exuded. His confident charisma was an exciting thing to watch, and she could tell by the way the two men at his side regarded him that he inspired their complete and total trust.

She glanced over at Roxanne, who was staring hungrily at him. No wonder she had such a fixation on Ty. It was perfectly understandable, she mused as her eyes wandered back to the magnetic man leaning casually in the doorway, laughing easily and making small talk with the potential client.

"Ste-eerike the bum out!" Helga roared, leaping up in her seat and sending her tub of popcorn flying. "What the hell are you lookin' at, Ump?"

Heartburn flaming, Ty ignored his mother and, catching Emily's eye, motioned her over to his side. Kissing her lightly on her cheek, he said, "Sweetheart, you already know Uncle Denny."

Uncle Denny, the soul of gentility, kissed the hand she extended. "Always a pleasure to see you, dear. And I'm so delighted that you could bring your mother, Tyler." He looked fondly over at Helga, who hung out the window to better threaten the umpire.

Wincing at the string of expletives coming from his fanatical parent, Ty valiantly carried on with the introductions. "And this is his guest—and longtime family friend—Mr. Brubaker, from Texas. Mr. Brubaker owns controlling interest in several very large companies that are looking to expand their software capabilities."

A diminutive man in a giant, ten-gallon cowboy hat stepped forward and enthusiastically pumped Emily's hand. "Wall, hello theah!" he bellowed, his eyes twinkling. "Nice to meetcha. And don't be givin' me any of that Mr. Brubaker crap, pardon my French." He doffed his hat at Emily and squinted at Ty. "Call me Big Daddy, little gal. Everybody does."

"Thank you, er, Big Daddy. I'll do that." Emily smiled down at the irresistible man, who stood no higher than her shoulder.

As Ty led her back to her seat, Big Daddy settled into the chair directly behind Emily and immediately struck up a conversation.

"So. I heah y'all are newlyweds! Congratulations! Boy howdy, theah's nothin' I like better than a weddin'." Pounding Ty manfully on the back, he winked broadly at him and said, "Looks to me like you made out, Ty, old boy. She's a beaut!"

Roxanne, seated next to Big Daddy and behind Ty, snorted in disgust.

"I'm a real family man, myself," the tiny Texan thundered in an effort to be heard above the enthusiastic crowd. "That's why I love doin' business with Denny and his niece. Did I mention that I have nine kids?" he asked as he fished the biggest wad of pictures out of his pocket that Tyler had ever seen.

"Wow, honey. Imagine that." Ty put a casual arm around Emily and squeezed. "Nine kids. Sounds like fun, doesn't it?"

Emily's eyes nearly bugged out of her head. "For you, maybe."

Disregarding her lack of enthusiasm, Ty laughed indulgently. "We want a big family ourselves," he confided to his potential client. "Isn't that right, hon?"

Another disbelieving snort came from Roxanne as she recrossed her legs, thumping Tyler roughly on the back of his head. "Sorry," she murmured in her smoky, bedroom voice.

Unable to stop herself, Emily shot an annoyed look at her husband's pushy boss. "Why, yes, darling, a big family," she agreed, and as though suddenly remembering that this was only an act, smiled brightly over her shoulder at Big Daddy and Roxanne. "*Big* family. Carmen wants lots of brothers and sisters, don't you, sweetheart?"

"*¡Sí! Muy grande familia! Sí!*" She clapped excitedly.

Roxanne shook her head, rolled her heavily made-up eyes toward the ceiling, and sighed the sigh of a woman condemned to a boring ball game with a bunch of tiresome ninnies.

As Emily chatted with the effusive Big Daddy, Ty glanced over to make sure his mother hadn't managed to get him fired yet. So far, so good, he mused, watching the usually mild-mannered Uncle Denny shout with glee at the umpire.

"Buddy, you're so blind your glasses need glasses!" the red-faced Denny hollered.

Helga roared. Punching Denny in the arm, she crowed, "Good one, Denny, old boy!"

Ty reached into his pocket and pulled out his extra-large bottle of industrial-strength antacid tablets and, pouring himself a handful, proceeded to eat them like candy. Helga's crude manners and boisterous behavior would certainly be the death of him. Never mind that Denny seemed somewhat amused by her antics. That would surely come to a grinding halt the moment she burst forth with a string of obscenities. Or perhaps she would pull the liner out of yonder garbage can and put on a fashion show that poor old Uncle Denny would never forget.

Popping another tablet into his mouth, Tyler decided to ignore the rowdy faction to his left and concentrate on wooing the client. After all, that's what he was here for. Turning his back on his lunatic mother, he glanced over at Emily, who was discussing the importance of family with Big Daddy Brubaker.

Her smile was so warm and genuine as she nodded in agreement with something the small Texan was pontificating about. Ty couldn't help but compare her graceful countenance with that of the brassy Roxanne. And seeing them in the same room together only drove the point further home.

She was doing a great job. Ty sat, momentarily lost in his ruminations. It was obvious that both Big Daddy and Uncle Denny thought she was wonderful, and even though Roxanne seemed skeptical, he was sure she could find no fault in his wife's performance.

He was even beginning to believe their story himself. In fact, he thought, noticing the smooth curve of her cheek lift slightly as she smiled, she seemed so authentic she almost made up for Helga's nutty behavior. An outburst from the old woman drew his eyes. Well, almost.

Emily was everything he could ever have asked for in a weekend wife. Hell, a forever wife even. Lovely. Gracious. Caring. His thoughts drifted to last night's episode in the pool. Sexy. Passionate. Hot. Eyes glazing over—as he recalled the incredibly vivid vision of her in that teensy bandage she called a swimsuit—his head lolled back in his seat. Maybe she would be up for another swimming lesson tonight, he mused. Provided he was still alive after an evening with the cast of *Cuckoo's Nest*.

The crowd's roar was only so much background noise as Ty began to envision himself stranded on a desert island with Emily. No Roxanne. No Uncle Denny. No Helga. Just the two of them and that itty-bitty, teensy-weensy, neon pink bikini.

"Looks like it's just the two of us," Roxanne leaned forward in her chair and whispered softly to Ty.

Still lost in his fantasy, Ty nodded happily. "Hmm?"

"Everyone else is ignoring us, silly," she cooed, tugging on a lock of hair at the back of his head. "It's just you and me."

"Oh." Tyler sat up abruptly, suddenly back at Dodger Stadium. For crying out loud. Couldn't he even attend a client meeting—with his wife and child, no less—without Roxanne coming on to him?

Was it time for a display of newlywed behavior with Emily? he wondered as his boss tickled the back of his neck with her long bloodred nails. Maybe a little husbandly kiss. Roxanne dug her nails in. Maybe a big honeymoon kiss. His blood ran warm at the thought. But wouldn't that seem tacky in the middle of a business meeting? Tough. It would be no tackier than the nympho seated behind him. Besides, he thought as Roxanne raked her claws down the back of his neck, he was getting desperate.

Hmm . . . How was he going to kiss Emily when she was still yapping away with the client? This could be tricky. He turned in his seat, trying to catch her eye. Just what the heck were they talking about, anyway?

"Extra mustard?" Emily was asking the Texan.

"Pour it on, honey pie! And ribs. See if they have some of those, will you?" Big Daddy nudged Roxanne playfully. "I can make a real mess with a pile of ribs."

Roxanne grimaced, and tried to hide the pained expression that crossed her face with a phony smile.

Emily reached out and twined her fingers through Tyler's. "Honey, I'm going to need some help gathering up all this food, would you mind coming with me?"

"No! Of course not, darling! I'd *love* to help." Leaping to his feet, he bolted to the door.

"Good." She looked strangely at him, and then turned to Carmen. "You be a good girl for Grandma, okay?"

"Don't worry about her, darlin'," Big Daddy instructed. "We'll keep an eye on her, won't we, Roxanne, honey?"

Roxanne took a large swig of her drink.

The grip Ty had on her hand threatened to squeeze the lifeblood out of her fingers as he pulled her roughly through the crowd to the lower-level concession stands. Dodging and weaving, his square jaw tightly clenched, he yanked her behind him until he found the farthest hot-dog stand he could find from their seats. Looking over his shoulder from time to time, as though the hounds of hell were hot on his trail, he battled his way toward the last and longest line.

Gasping for air, Emily reared back on his hand and dug her heels in. "Would you please slow down?" she pleaded, and attempted to adjust the skirt that had bunched so unattractively between her legs.

"Sorry," he mumbled, pausing while she pulled herself together.

Puzzled, Emily studied the pensive expression in his eyes. "What's the matter? I thought everything seemed to be going all right back there."

"It is." He sighed, leading her to a place at the end of the line. "It's just that she's still coming on to me."

"Can't you do something?"

"What? Challenge her to a duel? She's my boss, for crying out loud."

"I see your point. Besides, as your wife, that should probably be my job," she teased, trying to bring a smile back to his handsome face.

Ignoring the interested stares of the people waiting in line around them, Ty put a grateful arm around her shoulders and kissed the top of her head. "You'd do that for me?"

"Her choice of weapons. At dawn."

Ty beamed down at her sunny face. "You're doing a great job, you know. The client seems taken with you."

"Well… Uh… I wouldn't exactly say I was doing a *great* job." Lifting an insolent eyebrow, she stared back at a snoopy woman in a polyester jumpsuit who was standing in front of them and drinking in their every word. Turning her back on the nosy old broad, she sought out Ty's eyes, and decided there was no time like the present to fess up to the truth.

Concerned, Ty returned her gaze. "What's wrong?"

"Roxanne thinks I know Spanish. I can understand Carmen pretty well, but that's because she throws some English in every once in a while. But now Roxanne wants me to translate for her when we get to Mexico next week. Tyler, I've never been to Mexico before in my life!" She looked up at him, her eyes suddenly wide with fear.

The nosy woman in polyester swung her fascinated gaze over to Ty for his reaction.

"I don't suppose you speak any Spanish?" he asked hopefully.

"Not unless you count being able to ask where the train station is," she admitted lamely.

"Hmm. My Spanish is limited to ordering beer. Not really handy." Ty plowed a frustrated hand through his hair. "Unless we want to take her to the train station and get her drunk." He looked comically over at her.

The thought tickled her funny bone. "Hey, now. You might just be on to something there."

"Anything else you need to tell me?" Ty eyed her dubiously.

"No, honey. Only that I have to learn Spanish before next week."

Ty arched a worried eyebrow.

Emily shrugged resignedly. "I just don't know how you've stood that witch for so long," she said, exasperated after only part of an evening.

"And I've only been on the job for three days." He sighed and drew her possessively to his side.

"That's two and a half days too long, if you ask me," she huffed. "She is really awful. I'm sure there must be some kind of law against people like her."

"Probably, but I don't want to resort to that unless I have to. Uncle Denny is a super guy, and I really don't want to do anything that would hurt him, if I can avoid it. If you keep doing such a great job as my wife, hopefully we can." Rubbing her shoulders affectionately, he bent down and kissed her on the neck, behind the ear. "Just rehearsing," he whispered, nuzzling her earlobe with his nose.

"Oh. Uh, sure," she said breathlessly as his lips traveled lower. Too bad it wasn't for real, she mused, leaning back and tilting her head to give him access to the place where her neck met her shoulder.

Feeling as though he was being watched, Ty glanced up and winked at the still-gaping snoop in polyester. Then he pulled Emily into his arms for a heart-stopping kiss on the mouth. When he released her, the woman in line was fanning herself with her program.

"What was that for?" Emily whispered against his cheek as he held her tightly in his arms.

He kissed her lightly on the lips, her nose, her eyelids.

"Several reasons," he breathed, dancing her forward in line, nearly knocking over their spectator. "Partly for her benefit." He nudged the woman's polyester-clad shoulder. "Partly for rehearsal." He kissed her lips again. "But mostly for myself. I'm sorry." His arms tightened around her waist. "I know I promised to be a good boy, but—" his voice grew husky in her ear "—I've wanted to do that again ever since last night."

"Really?" Emily sighed, intoxicated by the feelings he set to life in her.

"Mmm-hmm." His low voice turned her knees to water.

"What'll it be, ma'am?" The teenager behind the counter reached out and tugged at the woman in polyester.

"I'll have a cot dog and a hoke," she replied, watching in fascination as Emily and Tyler continued to rehearse the more physical aspects of their act.

"I had a wonderful time tonight," Emily whispered into the darkened interior of Ty's Mercedes as they sped down the freeway toward home. And it was true. She couldn't remember a time when she'd enjoyed herself more. Carmen, tuckered out from an evening of hot dogs and candy and silver dollars from Big Daddy Brubaker, was sleeping soundly in the back seat next to the loudly slumbering Helga.

"Me, too." Ty looked surprised by his admission. Emily knew that he was exceedingly relieved to have the stressful evening over and done with. Everyone had managed to live through the ordeal, and even seemed to have had some fun in the process. "I think Big Daddy is going to go with Connstarr."

"Really?" Emily squeaked as loudly as she dared. "Did he say that?"

"No." He shook his head. "It's just a gut feeling I have. We spent a lot of time talking over that pile of ribs you brought him during the second half of the game. He's a pretty shrewd businessman, and I think he knows that Connstarr is the only realistic choice for him. But you know what I think really clinched the deal in his mind?'' He peered over at her face, dimly lit by the console.

"No. What?"

"You."

"Me?"

"I'm serious. He really liked you. He told me."

"Really?" Emily felt suddenly bashful.

"Yes. He said, and I quote, 'I love how gaga you two are over each other. Reminds me of me and the little missus down at the ranch.'''

Emily giggled. "He said that?"

"Honest. Thought we were gaga over each other."

Embarrassed, she suddenly occupied herself by checking on Carmen in the back seat. Big Daddy had hit just a little too close to home on the gaga issue. If she didn't get her emotions under control pretty soon, she would be in serious trouble. It was just that tonight had felt so right. She found herself wishing that she truly was Mrs. Tyler New-roth, and that Carmen was their daughter, and that Helga was her mother-in-law. A loud snort from the back seat brought her to her senses.

There she went again, fantasizing about something that she had no business even contemplating. It was becoming increasingly difficult to remember why she'd come to L.A. She had to stop thinking about how perfectly wonderful Ty was, and focus. Focus, focus, focus. But it was so hard, she thought as her eyes landed and focused on him.

"I think they had a good time, too," she commented, gesturing to the back seat and forcing herself to concentrate on something else.

Tyler chuckled to himself. "I've never seen anyone get into a seventh-inning stretch the way Mom did. The old 'Take Me Out to the Ball Game' song will never be the same in my mind," he said, referring to Helga's lusty caterwauling. She'd insisted on leading the group in song with her off-key screeches, while standing on her chair and waving her arms as if attempting to take flight.

"Yeah." Emily laughed. "But wasn't it worth it just to see the look of horror on Roxanne's face?"

Ty hooted. "Yep. Although my favorite part was when the Dodgers won and Helga broke one of the boss lady's claws trying to high-five her."

"Oh, stop!" Emily howled, tears of laughter beginning to run down her cheeks. "The look on her face."

"I thought she was having a seizure there for a second, her face seemed to catch fire."

Emily leaned against the passenger door and giggled until she couldn't stand it anymore. Lowering her window, she gulped in great lungfuls of fresh air, and attempted to pull herself together.

"I can't wait for the cruise," Ty declared. "I think Mom is really our secret weapon against Roxanne, after all."

"Ohh..." Emily groaned, falling into another paroxysm of laughter. Wiping at her watery eyes with the back of her hand, she thought about what he'd just said. Yes, indeed. He was almost certainly right. Helga and Roxanne stuck together on the same small ship should make for a fascinating cruise.

Chapter Seven

"Wow! If this is a deluxe cabin, I can only imagine what the commoners must be doing down in the basement," Emily joked, trying to figure out how she was going to maneuver past Ty to the pile of luggage stacked next to the couch that was to double as his bed.

"I don't know," he growled playfully, grabbing her by the waist as she attempted to squeeze by him in the tight confines of the ship's small cabin. "What are we going to do with all this room?"

"Let's have the Connstarr management team over for a dance," she quipped, glancing around at their cramped quarters, grateful that she didn't have to spend too much time in here alone with Ty.

"Great idea." He nodded and danced her backward toward the tiny area in front of the couch. "Just five or six hundred of our closest friends. Then again, I suppose I could invite the boss over to kill some time."

"It's your funeral," she replied lightly, and shifted in his arms to better see his face. "I wish we could have gotten adjoining cabins with Helga and Carmen. As it is, I have to sneak three doors down the hallway just to get to my own bed." Pursing her lips in frustration, she sighed as Tyler, humming happily, waltzed her in a two-foot square.

"Practice," he explained as he put her through her paces. "Just another one of those things we'll be expected to know how to do together. Anyway," he continued, returning to the subject at hand, "you could stay in here with me. That would solve several problems." Ty wiggled his eyebrows up and down playfully.

Emily pushed herself out of his embrace and laughed. "Yeah, right." And create several new ones. Focus, focus, focus, she reminded herself. "I suppose," she said, looking down at her sundress and high-heeled sandals, "that I should go change my clothes. What are we doing next?"

Wandering over to the couch, Tyler picked up the day's activity log and scanned it for things to do. Settling his long frame as comfortably as he could on the small couch, he said, "Let's see . . . Sunday, July 31. What time is it?" He glanced at his watch. "At one o'clock, we set sail. That's only a few minutes away. After that, at one-thirty, there's a compulsory lifeboat drill for all passengers."

"Really?" Emily sank down beside him on the couch and nervously gnawed the inside of her cheek. So far, so good, on the seasickness thing. But they weren't moving yet, either. The very thought of jumping into a lifeboat and drifting aimlessly out to sea in an emergency struck terror into her heart.

"Yeah." A look of concern crossed his face as he noticed the whitish pallor of her cheeks. Hastening to reassure her, he said, "Hey, don't worry, sweetheart. It's just a drill. They have to do it by law."

Emily took a deep breath to steady her nerves. Coming on this cruise had been a bad idea. Why was she here again? she wondered, glancing around the deluxe death trap they called a cabin. To risk her life out in the middle of the ocean...for what? Her thesis project? What the hell had she been

thinking when she chose this topic? It didn't even make
sense anymore. For heaven's sake, how was she supposed to
study the plight of the homeless from a lifeboat? She'd
rather take her chances on the street anyday. At least there
she didn't have to worry about sharks and drowning and...

Was it too late to get off this tub? They hadn't even left
the dock in San Diego yet, and already she was a wreck.

"Uh, Ty?" she asked feebly.

"Hmm?" he asked, looking up from the log. Cocking his
head to the side, he studied her panicked expression.

"I'm scared," she admitted in a tiny voice.

"Oh, honey." He smiled sympathetically and drew her
into the reassuring circle of his arms. His voice was soothing as he pushed her bangs back out of her eyes. "What are
you afraid of?"

"Sharks?" Her brows puckered together earnestly.

Ty let his head fall back against the porthole behind him,
and his comforting laughter rumbled deep in his chest. She
snuggled her cheek against this solid, muscular wall and let
the steady beat of his heart calm her frayed nerves.

"Honey, the only shark on this boat is Roxanne. And
don't worry, I won't let her get you." He rubbed her back
and kissed the top of her head. Picking up the ship's daily
cruise log, he continued. "It's not so bad, really. Listen, it
says here, 'please proceed to your cabin and put on your life
jacket.' That's not too scary. Then, 'check your boat number and location, and go directly to your boat station during the drill.' A piece of cake." He shrugged. "Now, if we
could only find our boat station."

Emily moaned into the soft folds of his polo shirt. "We're
dead ducks."

"No, no. It tells us right here. 'Promenade Deck, starboard side.' Hmm...which side is starboard?"

"Aahhh..." She buried her face into his neck.

Ty grinned. "You know what I think you need?"

"What?"

"I think you need to come with me to the Prom Lounge and hear 'the magical musical style of the Enchanted Cruise Tones, as they play for your listening pleasure.'"

"Yuck."

"Look. Right here." He pointed at the program. "It's either that or Lou Lewis and the Swinging All-Stars on the Disco Deck."

"Double yuck." She giggled.

"Hey, I don't write the program. I just read it," he said, looking injured. "So. What'll it be?"

She lifted her shoulders in a resigned shrug. "The lifeboat drill, I guess." Discussing death at sea seemed preferable to certain death at the musical hands of Lou Lewis. "But," she whispered, tilting her chin up on his chest and grinning, "let's not tell Roxanne."

Taking in a quick, deep breath, Ty stared at Emily in mock horror. "And risk losing Roxanne at sea? You're naughty." He grinned. "I like that in my women."

"Roxanne's naughty."

"No, Roxanne's evil. Big difference."

Smiling, she reached down and pulled her luggage next to her feet. "In any event, I suppose we should put our suits on under our shorts, that way after the drill, we can all catch some rays out at the pool."

"So you think you're ready to try out the pool in front of the Connstarr general public?" he asked, leaning down to help her with the clasp on her suitcase.

"Mmm-hmm," she mumbled as she rummaged around for her swimsuit. Heavens. She certainly ought to be. Between the extensive swimming and Spanish lessons during the last week, she should be able to accompany Jacques Cousteau on a diving expedition to Spain. Never had she crammed for any test the way she'd crammed for this one. And it had been fun. Tyler was an exceptionally patient instructor, teaching her and Carmen the rudiments of swimming.

Carmen had adored the lessons, taking to the water like a duck, in her little orange polka-dot swimsuit. Arms wound tightly around his neck, she'd giggled and splashed and basically fallen in love with Tyler, and Emily had the distinct impression that the feeling was mutual.

Helga, on the other hand, already knew how to swim, and lustily practiced her own technique. Attacking the water like a bulldog, she'd paddled around the deep end for a while, then hoisted herself up to the pool edge, where she'd beached her rotund body and shouted instructions at everyone else.

The Spanish came somewhat more easily than the swimming lessons for Emily. Much of her high school Spanish came back to her as she'd practiced her language tapes with Ty and Carmen.

Ty spent every moment that he was not at the office with them. The entire week had passed in a flurry of lessons, shopping for the cruise and practicing to be a family. Emily couldn't remember when she'd had so much fun. Helga and Carmen both positively basked in the attention and healthy life-style Ty provided. And Emily...well, she knew that with each passing day, she was getting in deeper trouble emotionally with Ty.

Finally discovering the sexy black bikini that had Ty's eyes bugging that first shopping day, she pulled it out of her suitcase and shut the lid. If she was going to compete with the ultra-sophisticated Roxanne, she had to fight fire with flare.

"I'll run down to Carmen and Helga's room and make sure they're ready to go," she said, stuffing the wispy black suit into the pocket of her sundress. "I can change down there with them."

"Better hurry." Ty nodded, diving into his own case and searching for his suit. "We sail in about two minutes."

"No problem. I told Helga to pop Carmen into her suit and have her ready for the playroom at the Kiddie Korner." Carmen had taken one look at the large play area and pool for children as they'd embarked, and pleaded to be allowed to go there first. "We can drop her by after—" She stopped talking and tilted her head in the direction of the door. "Ty!" she whispered, motioning for him to join her at the door. "Doesn't that sound like Roxanne?"

Peeking through the peephole, Tyler nodded. "It is her. And it looks like she's giving some poor slob from the purser's office hell."

The bitchy tones of Tyler's brassy boss reached them through the door as they stood huddled together listening to her tantrum.

"I don't care who's in there! I want them out!" she demanded, pointing at the room directly across from the Newroth cabin and stomping her foot. "I paid good money to get this particular cabin, and this is the cabin I shall have!"

"But, ma'am..."

"Don't 'but, ma'am' me!" she snapped. "It's obvious you don't know who I am." Fumbling in her massive purse, she dug out a business card and flung it at the puzzled purser. "Who was the young man I slipped the money to? I want to talk to him immediately."

"Wow," Emily breathed, looking up at Ty with wide eyes. "She bribed somebody on the crew to get the room across from you! We could have bribed someone to get an adjoining room for Helga and Carmen. Darn. Why didn't we think of that?"

Ty blew a disgusted puff of air between his lips. "Because our minds don't work like hers." Looking down at her, he shook his head. "I don't think you should go out there just yet," he advised, and turned back to peer through the hole in the door.

"I have to. I can't get dressed in here."

"Why not?"

Glancing around at the walls that seemed to physically close in and push her up against Tyler, she said, "Because it's too crowded."

"I hate to tell you this—" Ty's lips curved wryly "—but there isn't any more room down the hallway in Mom's room."

"Yes, but . . . I need to check on Carmen."

"Mom will take care of Carmen," he mumbled against the door as he strained to see what was happening in the hall.

"Yes, but they're girls down there."

Tyler shot a confused look over his shoulder at her. "Yeah. So?"

Feeling her cheeks begin a slow burn, she pushed her hand into the pocket of her sundress and fingered the black wisp that was her swimsuit. "I would just feel more comfortable getting dressed down there."

"Shh!" Ty stood and listened to the escalating sounds coming from the hallway. "I can't believe her." He shook his head, incredulous at the language filtering in from the hall. "Mom could take cussing lessons from Roxanne."

"Ty, I . . ."

"No." He sighed in exasperation. "Emily, I promise I won't look. Go into the bathroom and change if I make you nervous."

"But it's even more cramped in there."

"How much room do you need to put on a swimsuit? Especially that skimpy little thing." The tiny smile lines at the corners of his eyes crinkled in amusement.

Emily shrugged miserably. "Um, a lot."

Comprehension slowly crossed Ty's face. "You're not claustrophobic, too, are you?"

"Sort of. Just when I'm on a boat, actually." Looking down at the straps of her high-heeled sandals, she wished the floor would open up and swallow her alive. Usually, Emily fancied herself to be a hearty, well-adjusted woman of emotional substance. As long as she was in a big room on dry land. However, between her fear of drowning and her fear of closed-in spaces, she was beginning to wonder if they were going to have to carry her off the ship in a strait-jacket. Ty probably thought she was a real case.

Smiling softly, he shook his head and chuckled. "What am I going to do with you?"

"Fire me?" she asked timidly.

"Fire the little woman? Don't be silly." Scratching his head, he glanced at his watch. "Look, we're setting sail any second now. Why don't I wait in the bathroom, while you change into your suit out here where there's more room?"

Flashing him a relieved smile, she nodded and opened the bathroom door for him. "I'll only be a second," she promised as he stepped inside.

Ty retreated into his bathroom and, flipping the lid down on the commode, settled in for a wait. As he listened to the rustling sounds of his wife changing her clothes, he propped his elbows on his knees and rested his chin in his hands. She was so cute, he thought, grinning. He couldn't think of a single thing that he didn't like about her. Even her irrational fears. And, considering she'd almost drowned as a young girl, those fears really weren't irrational. Actually, he admired the way she was able to overcome her emotions and learn to swim last week.

He could hear her humming an off-key tune through the door as she dressed in the sexy, formfitting black suit that had nearly given him an embolism that day in the department store. He couldn't wait to show her off out at the pool. It was a pretty safe bet that there wasn't another Connstarr wife who could touch her in the looks department. Or the genuinely nice department ... or the sexy department. ...

He could have spent months searching for the perfect woman to play his wife, and never found one more suited to his needs than Emily. It was incredible how different she and Roxanne were. The two—thankfully—were night and day.

Emily stripped down to her underpants, and froze. What was that? It sounded like someone was rattling a door-knob. Ty wouldn't be coming out already, would he? She narrowed her eyes at the bathroom. No, there it was again.

Shifting her glance to the cabin door, she saw the knob slowly move. What the...?

Snatching her sundress off the floor, she wrapped it around the front of her body and padded quietly over to the door in bare feet. She tiptoed up to the peephole and gasped. Roxanne's fearsome bustline filled her view.

"Ty!" she gasped, spinning around and tapping on the bathroom door.

"All dressed?" he asked eagerly as he started to push open the door.

"No!" she squeaked, slamming the door on his fingers.

"Ow!"

"Sorry... " Adjusting the drooping sundress to better cover her modesty, she pushed her lips to the open crack in the bathroom door. "Ty! Roxanne is trying to come into our room!"

"*What?*" he called as he poked through the cabinet, searching for a bandage. "What does she want?"

"You, of course!" There was a loud rap at the front door. "Ty! She wants in! I'm not dressed! What should I do?"

"Here, I'll handle this." Exasperated, Ty pushed the bathroom door open and, with his eyes closed, stumbled out to where Emily was standing. Waving his arms in front of him like a sleepwalker, he pointed his head in the direction he thought she was standing and reassured her. "Don't worry, I can't see anything."

"That's obvious." She giggled as he spoke confidentially to the lamp.

"Oh." He turned at the sound of her voice and shrugged sheepishly. "Point me toward the door, will you?" Thrusting his hands out in front of him, he swung in a half circle where he found and groped her face. "Is that you?" he whispered teasingly.

"No!" She laughed, pulling his thumb out of her mouth. "It's Roxanne, and I bite."

"Very funny," he snickered in hushed tones as he tugged on a lock of her hair. "Are you sure you're not decent? This is ridiculous."

Her eyes dropped to the skirt of her sheer sundress that she held to shield her half-naked body. "I'm sure."

"How about if I just open one eye?" he whined, feeling his way down her head to her smooth, bare shoulder. "Hmm..."

Another loud rap at the door.

"Who is it?" he called, tightening his grip on Emily's shoulder as she shook with laughter.

"Tyler? It's me, Roxanne," she purred through the door. "Can I come in?"

"Uh, Roxanne? We'd love to have you in, but my wife is standing here naked...hem." He coughed as Emily punched him in the ribs.

Tightening her sundress across her near nudity, she leaned over to Tyler. "That's not true!" She giggled nervously.

"It's not? Then you won't mind if I open my eyes," he whispered, sliding his hand down her bare back.

Gasping, she slithered out of his grasp. "You better not!" Her giddy laughter was louder than she'd intended.

"What's going on in there?" Roxanne demanded.

Her mouth twisting in annoyance, Emily tugged on Tyler's shirt. "Tell her it's none of her damn business," she huffed. "No." She wiggled between Tyler and the door. "I'll tell her!"

Clamping a large hand over her mouth, Ty whispered, "Easy, tiger," and opened his eyes. Unable to control himself, his glance shot down to check the state of her undress.

Catching him in the act, she tried to protest, her muffled screeching traveling no farther than his palm.

"Quiet." He chuckled. "She'll think you're trying to give me another black eye, and try to come to my rescue."

"Mmm-mmm-hmm!"

As she swirled her tongue around the inside of his palm, he began to laugh. "Would you quit it?" he demanded as the tickling sensations she lavished wetly across his palm and between his fingers drove him slowly out of his mind. "I mean it, Em!" he growled, hauling her up against his body and pulling the delicate shell of her ear into his mouth. "You'd better quit while you're ahead."

"Tyler?" Roxanne called impatiently.

"Yeah?" he answered in a strangled voice.

Tapping an irritated nail on the door, she barked, "The Connstarr management team, which includes you, by the way, and accounts for over half the passengers on this tub, will be meeting topside in about two minutes to throw confetti and drink champagne and have fun! I will expect you and your wife there, *immediately!*" Her voice rose shrilly, revealing her annoyance at being kept out of his cabin.

"Yes, ma'am," Ty drawled. "We're nearly finished in here."

"Good," she snapped after a moment's pause, and then, not wanting to miss the fun, the echo of Roxanne's indignant heels faded away as she marched down the hallway.

"Think she's mad?" Emily giggled as Tyler pulled his hand away from her mouth.

Shrugging, Tyler kissed the minx he still held in his arms on the side of the head. "Who cares?" he asked, shocked to find that for the first time since he'd arrived on the West Coast, he could relax.

"I suppose it would be useless to ask if she has to wear that," Ty grumbled resignedly as they wove their way through the Connstarr throng toward the three remaining empty lounge chairs by the pool.

Emily glanced over her shoulder at Helga and grinned. The lopsided straw hat piled high with plastic fruit had caught the older woman's fancy in the gift shop window. Unable to resist the longing in her eyes, Emily had talked Ty into buying it.

"Are you kidding?" she asked under her breath as Ty nodded and waved at the different Connstarr bigwigs they passed. "Just be thankful it's this and not the plastic shower cap she was planning on wearing in the pool."

"I guess," he muttered as he called a cheery hello to a department head from the Detroit branch. Draping a casual arm around Emily's waist, he wore the look of a proud and protective husband, propelling his beautiful wife toward her seat. "After we settle in here for a few minutes, I'd like to introduce you to a few people. Feel up to that?"

"Amazingly enough, I feel great. Those patches must be working. So I guess I'm as ready as I'll ever be..." Mingling was something she was pretty good at. Not one to be intimidated by a strange social crowd, she could usually plunge in and make pointless small talk with the best of them. But this was going to be much trickier than her usual collegiate gathering. Now she was a middle-class student posing as a homeless waif, who was acting as a socialite. How would she ever keep the three faces of Em straight? Her expression clouded with uneasiness.

Patting her waist affectionately, Ty dropped a newlywed kiss lightly on her lips. "Don't worry," he whispered, giving her a conspiratorial wink. "I'm here for you, pumpkin."

And she knew deep down in her heart that it was true. As long as she needed him, he would be there for her. Pausing at her lounge chair, Emily was surprised to discover that she completely trusted him, without reserve. In the past week an invisible bond had begun to form between her and Ty, binding them together and taking root in her heart. She would never forget Tyler Newroth's kindness, and hoped that years after they'd gone their separate ways, they would still keep in touch.

"Sure," she said, looking up at her handsome new husband with her best newlywed expression of adoration. "I'd love to meet some of your co-workers."

He answered her adoring gaze with a look so piercing it stole her breath away. Though it was impossible to tell what he was thinking in that brief moment, Emily had the disquieting feeling that he was not as at ease with this act as he appeared to be.

Coloring, she averted her eyes and tossed her beach towel down on the lounge chair. "I, uh, think I'll go for a quick dip," she announced, and stepped out of her shorts and top, revealing the black suit she'd saved for the cruise.

"Good idea," Ty agreed, running a hand over the tense muscles of his jaw. "A nice cold swim is just what I need."

As Ty pulled his T-shirt off over his head, Emily could feel the sea of female eyes that surrounded the pool—disguised by dozens of pairs of expensive sunglasses—zero in on her husband's powerful build. This past week of swimming lessons had turned his smooth skin a beautiful shade of bronze. His well-muscled body moved with easy grace to the deep end, and these admiring women exchanged hungry glances.

Plunging neatly into the smooth surface of the water, he swam several laps, while Emily slipped into the shallow end and watched his fan club begin to salivate. Fighting irrational feelings of jealousy, she willed herself to remember that he was not her man ... and never would be.

Swimming easily to the metal stairs at the deep end, he shook the water from his face and pulled himself, with one fluid movement, out of the pool. His stance, hands planted firmly on narrow hips, broad shoulders square in silhouette, spoke of a man who had made it—in his mind and in the world. With a commanding air of self-confidence, he stood there, breathtakingly handsome, and lifted his upper lip in a lazy smile at his wife.

Sure that she would melt from the sheer heat of his look, Emily dived under the water's surface and stayed there until she couldn't hold her breath another second. Rising to the top, she scanned the deck for him, only to discover that he had gone to join Helga on the chairs. Valiantly, she tried to ignore the stab of disappointment she felt when he didn't spend some time playing with her in the pool, and focused instead on Roxanne, who, ever on the prowl, was making a beeline to where he sat.

Paddling slowly over to the edge of the pool, Emily watched in disgusted fascination as Roxanne boldly pushed Emily's beach towel off the chair next to Ty's and replaced it with her own. With much flamboyant preening, she finally settled down and, digging through her large beach satchel, came up with a bottle of baby oil.

"Ty, honey, I was just wondering if you'd mind putting some of this on me?" she asked breezily, thrusting the bottle of oil into his hand. "I can't always reach some of the more...delicate areas all by myself."

"I'm not surprised," Helga piped up, leaning across her son and gaping at Roxanne. "You've got a lot of southern exposure on the back forty there." Pushing her fruit-filled straw hat back from her eyes, she peered at the indignant woman's minuscule suit. "You call that a bathing suit?" Clucking her tongue, she rolled her eyes at Tyler and announced, "Looks like a piece of dental floss, the way it rides up her..."

"Mom!" Ty choked and coughed politely, attempting to stem the laughter that welled in his throat. "You haven't tested out the pool yet. Why don't you go join Em?" He pointed to Emily, who he'd noticed had had to duck under the water to stop from laughing.

"Okay." She waved an impatient hand at Tyler and offered the thoroughly insulted Roxanne another piece of her mind. "I wouldn't run around in that suit too much now, dearie. Why, that little string you're wearing could saw you right in two."

"Mom!" Ty was unsuccessful in his attempt to look sternly at Helga.

Roxanne's smile could not hide the venom behind her eyes as she gathered up her beach towel and satchel and nodded curtly at Helga. "Mrs. Newroth, enjoy your swim." Turning to Ty, she smiled provocatively. "I just remembered some unfinished business back in my cabin... I'll catch up with you later, when we can discuss our business in *private*." Setting her ample derriere in motion, she disappeared into the crowd.

Helga nudged Ty and nodded at the bottle of Roxanne's baby oil he still held in his hand. "As long as you're passing out massages, do me, sonny," she ordered, and flopped over onto her stomach.

Shrugging, Tyler grinned over at Emily, who—legs still dangling in the water—had propped herself on her elbows at the side of the pool. Their gazes locked for a supercharged moment, until Ty, winking lazily, turned his attention to his "mother."

Emily watched with smiling eyes as he good-naturedly oiled the nutty Helga, and suddenly realized, right then and there, that she was falling madly in love with her husband.

"Could I have this dance?" Ty whispered to Emily as the Enchanted Cruise Tones swung into a mellow ditty, just perfect for slow dancing.

Forgetting that she was merely putting on a show for the party at their dinner table, Emily nodded. She looked up into Ty's dark, heart-stoppingly sexy eyes, and felt her body elevate, of its own accord, up out of her chair and into his arms.

"Yes. I'd love that," she murmured. Slipping her arm around his waist, she followed him out to the dance floor.

His spicy aftershave filled her senses as she laid her head against the crisp, clean lines of his dinner jacket and began to sway with him to the music. No doubt about it, she mused, glancing around at the other diners in the Falling Star Dining Room reserved for Connstarr employees alone, he was definitely the best-looking man in the room. Probably even the entire boat, she gloated, and snuggled closer into her husband's embrace.

Who was she kidding? Eyes closed, she lay against Ty and had to remind herself yet again that he was not hers. A powerful man like Tyler Newroth could never be interested in a woman like her. Not seriously, anyway. She had the feeling that when Ty fell in love, it wouldn't be with a grungy woman he'd picked up at the side of the road. And if he were ever to discover that she was only posing as a homeless woman, how would he react to being lied to? Especially considering how generous and giving he'd been with her.

The thought of his displeasure at discovering the truth made her shudder involuntarily as they danced.

"Cold?" His warm breath tickled her ear.

"No," she whispered, not bothering to explain. What was there to tell? He would probably jump ship and swim back to L.A. if he even suspected that she was beginning to fall for him. She would just have to take each moment as it came with him, collecting memories of their brief but glorious time together to sustain her in her old age. After all, she still had a whole week to bask in her role as Mrs. Tyler Newroth. Why not enjoy it?

Today had certainly been wonderful. Helga had collected Carmen from the Kiddie Korner and taken her to their cabin for a nap, leaving Ty and Emily free to swim and get to know the Connstarr crowd. After mingling with and being introduced to more of the immense management team than she would ever be able to remember, they had joined some of Ty's friends from the Boston division in the lounge for happy-hour drinks and hors d'oeuvres. Unable to remember when she'd laughed so hard, Emily could see why he missed the crew on the East Coast.

Roxanne's arrival had broken up the little party and, making their excuses, the Newroths had retreated to their room to dress for dinner. Ty had been a doll and changed in the bathroom, allowing Emily the space she needed to comfortably slip into her strapless black dinner dress. Once she'd put the finishing touches on her hair and makeup, she hurried down the hallway to the room she shared with Helga and Carmen to check on them.

Connstarr had supplied a bevy of baby-sitters and a host of interesting things for the children of its staff to amuse themselves with. Carmen was more than content to spend the evening with her new little friends, watching movies and drawing pictures.

Helga, looking matronly in her formal attire, eagerly joined Emily and Tyler as they headed toward the dining room, hoping to catch a glimpse of Denny. As luck would have it, he had been seated at their dinner table with Roxanne when they'd arrived.

As crabby as Roxanne had been over Tyler's attentive behavior toward his bride during dinner, she had managed to behave herself, if only to please her uncle Denny. Not that Uncle Denny would have noticed one way or another. Much to the disgust of his niece and the amusement of Ty and Emily, he and Helga cavorted and carried on over their meal like a couple of giddy kids.

"How much do you think Roxanne had to pay the maître d' to get a seat at our table?" Ty asked, weaving Emily across the dance floor and slowly over to the door that led to the deck.

Emily giggled, loving the rumble of his deep voice as it resonated in his chest. "Whatever it takes. She certainly had no problem kicking the family across the hall from us out of their cabin and moving in."

"Now she can spy on us to her heart's content," Ty muttered.

"You know, in a way I kind of feel sorry for Roxanne." Emily sighed as Ty stopped dancing and looked down at her, a slow smile softening his features.

"You're too nice for your own good."

"Oh, I don't know," she mused, following Ty over to the railing where they could look out at the golden pink glow of the setting sun. The light, salty spray misted the air as the tropical breezes flirted with the sea. Emily lifted her face to the iridescent light and tried to capture forever the feelings of magic and wonder she felt at this moment. It was easy to feel compassionate when she felt so perfectly blissful herself. "Usually, when people act the way she does, there's a reason," she explained, turning her face up to Ty.

Pulling a stray tendril of hair away from her eyes, his mouth curved slowly in a tender smile. The look on his face was unbearably sweet, and Emily knew she would never forget the enchantment of this moment.

She came alive in his arms, this feeling of trancelike happiness carrying her to another place and time. A place where she could believe that she and Ty belonged together. A time where the passion-filled look he was bestowing on her was meant only for her and not for the benefit of an unwanted admirer.

Wrapping herself in the magic, she allowed herself to believe that he truly cared, and that the arms that tightened convulsively around her slender waist were her permanent refuge from the harsh realities of the world.

"You're so sweet," he murmured, tilting her chin up so that he could search for the key to her soul through her eyes. "I've never met anyone quite like you. It's amazing, really, that you've managed to remain so loving and understanding, in spite of everything." A smile of admiration tipped the corners of his mouth.

Emotions raged within her as she tried to mask a disquieting flash of guilt. If she could tell him the truth, she would, she assured herself, ignoring the warning voice in her head. The voice that cautioned her against giving herself to the moment. To Ty.

"No," she whispered, her eyes flashing, searching his for understanding. "I'm nothing special. Really." He had to know, if only on a subconscious level, that she was not some wonder woman from the streets, overcoming incredible odds to survive, but merely a grad student researching a project.

He angled her mouth up to his and, shaking his head, smiled. "To me, you are very special."

His kiss was electric, causing her stomach to jump wildly as he pushed her lips apart with his own. His insistent mouth demanded a response, and she found herself standing on tiptoe, straining to lose herself in his slow, mind-drugging kisses. Never before had she felt the dizzying sensations of desire coil so rapidly throughout her body.

Her pulse pounded at the base of her throat, under the gentle stroke of his thumb. Ever so slowly, he backed her up against the deck rail, pressing his thighs solidly into her hips. She settled back, reveling in the feel of his hands as they glided over her with almost unbearable tenderness.

Moaning softly into his mouth, she curled into the curve of his firm body, eliciting an immediate response from him.

His voice was unsteady as he spoke raggedly against her mouth. "If I'd had any idea that being married was anything like this..." He sighed, nibbling at her lower lip. "I'd have gotten married years ago."

"Me, too," she breathed lightly from between her parted lips.

"You are incredible." His gaze swept over her like the warm ocean breezes that softly riffled their hair. Nuzzling her neck, he pulled her away from the rail and into his arms. "Where did you come from?" he demanded, raining a trail of kisses down to the hollow of her throat. "What deep, dark secrets are you hiding from me?"

Letting her head fall back against the strength of his forearm, she shivered lightly and shrugged. These were questions she must not answer, she told herself, struggling to remember why she had made this rule in the first place. Who was she? Why was she there? These were good questions that even she didn't know the answers to anymore.

Tyler sighed and cradled her face in his hands, a look of quiet desperation in his eyes. "Just promise me you won't disappear at midnight."

Smiling, Emily opened her mouth to promise, but was cut short by Roxanne's sharp cry.

"There you are!" she shouted gaily, sashaying down the deck toward them. Tapping Emily on the shoulder, she purred prettily, "May I cut in?"

Chapter Eight

Tyler closed his eyes against the tide of frustration that urged him to throw his boss over the ship's railing without a life preserver. As ever, her timing was incredible.

"Hello, Roxanne," Ty practically growled as he struggled to keep a civil tongue in his head. He had much more pressing matters to attend to than spending useless time with the barracuda he called "boss." Tightening his grip on Emily's waist, he did his best to swallow his impatience. Maybe they would be lucky and she would leave. Or jump ship. Or drop dead. He didn't care as long as he could return to the ecstasy of Emily's embrace.

"What on earth are you two doing out here?" Her suspicious eyes flicked across Emily's pink cheeks and swollen lips with disdain. "The party is inside." Scolding, she tucked her hand into the crook of Ty's arm. "I think it would be a good idea if the two of us had a dance," Roxanne told Tyler, turning him away from Emily. "Political correctness and all that. You don't mind," she tossed over her shoulder at Emily.

"No?" Still dazed at having been so rudely jerked out of her dreamworld, Emily looked up at Ty for the answer.

Ty snorted in disgust as Roxanne tugged him toward the interior dance floor. It wasn't like she was giving either of them a choice. How could he possibly refuse without seeming like a complete heel? Shaking his head, he knew that part of his disgust was with himself for letting this big-haired bimbo run his life. Career future or no, it was time to damn the torpedoes and have a man-to-snake talk with his boss. Monday morning, bright and early, back at the office. Till then—for Uncle Denny's sake—he'd play nice.

Setting his jaw firmly, he turned and nodded at Emily. "I'll be back. Just . . . remember where we left off," he instructed, and with one last, clock-stopping grin, was yanked inside by Roxanne.

Just how many dances did it take to achieve political correctness? Emily wondered, listening to the strains of the Enchanted Cruise Tones as they pounded out yet another rousing ditty for their dancing pleasure. From where she sat next to the railing, the sounds of a party in the throes of a critical mass meltdown reached her ears.

As she sat shrouded in dusky twilight, a sense of melancholy settled over her, causing her to feel all alone in the world, even as she listened to the shrieks of laughter from the rowdy Connstarr crowd.

In a way, it was almost lucky that Roxanne had found them when she had, Emily reflected, trying to make some sense out of her relationship with Ty. What was happening to her? Why couldn't she stay emotionally detached? Other researchers could go undercover without getting all tied up in emotional knots. So what was wrong with her?

Sighing heavily, she watched the last vestiges of the sun disappear into the clear, blue Mexican Pacific, and felt a bit of herself drowning right alongside. Obviously she was not cut out for social work. Her poor heart would bleed to death over every case that came her way.

Except, of course, for Ty. Tyler Newroth had taken over her heart in a completely different way. A way that she had never experienced before in her life. A way that she could only classify as true love. She laughed to herself at the irony.

How many times had she sworn to her sister Erica that this was it? True love. And how many times had she been wrong? Wincing, she thought of her identical twin sister pointlessly coaxing along a love affair with Will Spencer for her up in Northern California. While she researched the homeless, Erica was wasting her time, unwillingly pretending to be Emily, so that Will would still be there for her when she got back.

Shoot, Emily thought, nibbling guiltily on the inside of her cheek. How would she ever be able to tell her sister that she didn't love Will, and that after meeting Tyler Newroth, now knew that she never would? Erica would probably kill her.

How ironic that the one man she'd found true love with should be the one man who could probably never fall in love with a grungy little street person he'd rescued from the side of the road. The one true hero left in this uncaring world. A man who had so generously given to three people in desperate need. Feeling a sudden and acute sense of loss over something she had never actually had, she swallowed, and tried to stem the flood of tears that pricked the backs of her eyes.

This was ridiculous, she chided herself. Here she was, mooning over something that had never really even existed outside of her own mind. Shaking off the mental anguish, and focusing on her true reason for being on this ship in the first place, she gripped the railing and pulled herself up and out of her chair. Gazing at the horizon, she spied a falling star and quickly made a wish. If she were lucky, and it came true, Helga and Carmen would never go hungry again.

Helga, having the time of her life, was leading a conga line across the floor as Emily slipped into the dining room and rejoined the party at their table. Face glowing a crimson shade of heart-attack red, Uncle Denny gripped Tyler's mother tightly around her waist and tossed his dignity to the trade winds.

The picture was so touching, Emily couldn't squelch the mirth that bubbled, unbidden, into her throat. Trust Helga to help her forget her troubles.

The tempo of the music changed and the conga line broke up, leaving only couples on the floor to slow dance. Noting the look of distress on Ty's face as Roxanne thrust her voluptuous body into his arms, Emily decided it was time to reclaim her husband. Roxanne had had him long enough.

Tapping Roxanne on the shoulder, Emily smiled politely and attempted to wedge her way between the two. "My turn," she announced airily as Ty stepped back from Roxanne and allowed her into the circle of his arms.

"All right," Roxanne snapped, pursing her lips in annoyance. "But the next slow dance is mine."

"I've got some money," Ty murmured gratefully into Emily's ear as he swept her to a far corner of the floor. "Maybe I can persuade the band to play 'Flight of the Bumblebee' for the rest of the evening."

Emily's buoyant laughter rang out, causing more than one head to turn and stare at the couple with envy. "That's definitely not slow-dance material," she teased. "I take it you don't enjoy dancing with Roxanne."

"Dancing? Is that what we were doing? I thought I was wrestling a bear in a gunnysack."

"That bad?" she squeaked, clutching his lapels as she laughed with delight.

"No-oo..." he said, feigning heavy thought. "Not that easy, actually. It was more like trying to steer a hefty bag of pudding around the floor. A hefty bag with lips."

"Lips?" Emily cried in mock anger. "Did she kiss you?"

"Tried."

"Really?"

Ty nodded and grinned. "But don't worry, honey. My virtue is still intact."

"Thank heavens." Emily sighed and leaned into his chest. "I didn't want to have to tear her hair out." She smothered a yawn into the back of her hand. "That would take all night."

Chuckling comfortably, he rubbed a gentle hand across her back, massaging her flesh through the thin material of her dress. "Sleepy?"

"Not anymore," she answered, arching against his heavenly hands and smiling up into his face.

"You can't fool me. I saw that yawn." Moving up her back, he eased the tension out of the muscles in her neck with a practiced hand. "I'm sorry I had to leave you out on the deck like that."

"Shh..." Emily shook her head and leaned back in his arms to better see him. "Hey, I know it wasn't your idea. You were smart to go with her. It was...politically correct." Her eyes twinkled with fun.

"Do you have any idea how hard it was for me to follow her in here and dance with her?"

Emily nodded shyly. "I think so." Her heart thudded erratically beneath her breast.

"Mmm," Ty murmured, and pulled her more firmly into his embrace.

Moving slowly around the room, mesmerized by each other's touch, both were unconscious of the change in musical tempo.

"Uh-oh."

"What's wrong?" Emily asked dreamily.

"Roxanne at twelve o'clock high, headed this way. No!" he commanded, whipping her around in his arms. "Don't look."

"Why not?" She giggled.

Ty blew an incredulous puff of air between his lips. "Obviously, you've never danced with that human water bed, or you'd know the answer to that."

"Sorry, dumb question."

"Why don't we just pretend we don't see her, and then you yawn really big, and I'll look all concerned and tell you we should call it a night?" Ty recommended, watching Roxanne thread her way toward them out of the corner of his eye.

"Okay, honey," she murmured and, lifting her chin, yawned broadly up at him.

"Very good," he praised under his breath. "Oh, honey," he said too loudly. "You look tired. I'm going to take you to bed right now." He darted a quick look down at Emily. "How'd that sound?"

"Nasty."

He grinned rakishly at her. "Good."

"Ty!" Emily was pacing fitfully around the minuscule living area of Ty's cabin.

"Would you please sit down?" he asked as he loosened his tie and shrugged out of his dinner jacket. "You're giving *me* motion sickness."

"Ty, I can't stay here all night." She paced over to the front door for the hundredth time and peeked through the peephole, across the hall to Roxanne's room. "I don't believe this. Her door is *still* open."

"I believe it," Ty put in dryly, tossing his tie onto the counter. "Walk-ins are probably welcome."

"You're terrible," she flung over her shoulder, but laughed in spite of herself. "I wonder what she's up to?" Her nose was beginning to ache from being pressed up against the door. Having followed Ty back to his room for propriety's sake, and spending the ten minutes it took to change into her newlywed negligee and brush her teeth, she was ready to relieve the sitter and join Carmen in their bed.

Unfortunately, Roxanne, who was either bored, suspicious, or both, had left the party and followed Tyler and his bride as they'd returned to their room, and slipped into her cabin across the hall. And, for some bizarre reason that

Emily couldn't fathom, had left her door wide-open. For more than an hour now, Emily had been trying to get back to the room she shared with Helga and Carmen without being spotted, which was virtually impossible the way Roxanne kept hovering around her doorway.

"Probably exactly what we think she's up to. Spying on us." Ty kicked off his shoes and swung his feet up onto the couch. "Em, honey, a watched pot never boils. Sit down and forget her, and she'll eventually close her door."

"Ah! Ahh... Ah-ha!" Emily smiled jubilantly at Tyler. "The pot boiled. I can go now." Tying her sash tightly around her waist, she smiled shyly. "Good night. I... had a great time."

"Me, too." Swinging to his feet, Ty crossed the room and took her loosely into his embrace. "A really great time. Good night," he murmured, kissing her lightly on the forehead. Opening the door, he led her out into the hallway. "See you in the mor—couple of minutes or so," he said blithely as Roxanne came bursting out of her cabin.

"Hello." Tyler's boss arched an inquisitive eyebrow at Emily, who stood self-consciously clutching at her negligee. "Going somewhere?" Her satisfied smile implied that she thought she had finally caught them at their little game.

"Yes, to check on my daughter. And you?" Emily asked smoothly, feeling Ty's gentle pat of admiration on her hip.

"Me?" Roxanne's laugh was phony. "Oh, just heard all the commotion in the hall and decided to check it out. You can't be too careful these days."

"Well, we'll try to keep it down." She smiled. Commotion? She must have been listening at her door with a stethoscope, Emily thought as Roxanne's beady eyes flitted back and forth between her and Ty.

Roxanne bared her teeth, Cheshire-style. "That would be nice. I'm just going to leave my door open for a few more minutes. It's so stuffy in these little cabins, don't you think?"

"We were just saying that ourselves, weren't we, darling?" Ty looped an affectionate arm around Emily's shoulders. "We were just in there steaming up the windows a few minutes ago, had a regular sauna cooking in there, huh, honey?"

Emily nodded dumbly and averted her gaze from the hostility that fairly radiated from Roxanne's narrowed eyes.

"Well, good night then, Roxanne," Ty called as his boss retreated into her room. In the same loud voice, he called after Emily, "Hurry back, sweetheart. I get so lonely without you."

"I'll just be a minute," she answered, and slipped into her own room. Once inside, she found Helga sitting on the edge of Carmen's bed, stroking the young girl's soft, dark curls. "When did you get back? I thought you were still out kicking up your heels with Uncle Denny."

Helga smiled up at Emily. "Just now. I let the sitter go." Glancing at Emily's negligee, she snorted. "Looks like you're the one who's been kicking up her heels."

"Nah, this is just my disguise."

"Yeah, yeah. It's a tough job, but somebody's got to do it, right?"

Emily blushed. "Actually, I can't stay. I have to go back to Ty's room until Roxanne shuts her door."

"Mmm-hmm."

Choosing to ignore Helga's skeptical grin, Emily picked up her journal and headed to the door. "Hopefully, I'll be back soon."

"Mmm-hmm."

"What are you doing?" Ty asked, watching Emily, who was curled up on the corner of the couch, scribble furiously in her notebook.

"I... Uh..." Pausing, she chewed the end of her pen. "I keep a diary. It... relaxes me."

"Roxanne's got you pretty uptight, huh?"

"I'm beginning to think she's going to leave her door open all night." There was no way she could spend the night in this room. Not after the kiss she'd shared with Ty out on the deck that evening. Suddenly even innocent time spent alone with him took on a whole new meaning in her mind.

"Nah. She'll get tired of snooping and close it." For lack of something better to do, he wandered to the door and peeped through the peephole.

"I hope so." Emily hugged her diary to her chest, glad that Ty had no idea what she'd just written there. She wouldn't solve anything by revealing her blossoming feelings toward him to anyone but her journal. Only disaster could spring from such a revelation. Complete and total disaster... for her thesis, for Carmen and Helga, for her fragile heart. No. Best to vent these thoughts to the private pages of her trusty journal. Then, someday, when she had recovered from the broken heart that was sure to come from loving and eventually losing Ty, she could destroy these pages without anyone ever being the wiser.

"Hey," he whispered. "The coast is clear. Roxanne shut her door and the hall is empty. Hurry." He beckoned to her with his hand.

Snapping her diary shut, Emily hopped up and sprang to the door. "Thanks," she whispered, feeling incredibly awkward again.

"No problem." Slowly opening the door, Ty poked his head out into the hallway and looked both ways. "Go!" he urged, nudging her quietly out the door.

With one last, backward glance, Emily shot out the door, down the hallway and straight into Uncle Denny, who, having just rounded the corner, stood poised to knock on Helga's door.

Darn. What was he doing here?

"Hello, Mr. Delmonico." Emily tugged at the hem of her revealing negligee.

Crimson-cheeked, Uncle Denny dropped his hand mid-knock. "Hello, my dear. I was...uh, just...looking for..."

The door opened and a beaming Helga reached out and grabbed Uncle Denny by the arm. "Denny, old boy! You're late." Tugging him into the room behind her, she looked expectantly at Emily. "We're gonna play a little five-card stud. Wanna play?"

"Uh, no, thanks. I just came to check on Carmen," she explained for Uncle Denny's benefit.

"The kid is fine. She's in the connecting bedroom, dead to the world," Helga assured her, impatient to get on with her date.

"Okay, then." She smiled limply at Uncle Denny. Under her breath, she muttered to Helga, "Don't take all night. Call me as soon as the coast is clear."

"Yeah, yeah."

"I mean it," she stressed as the door closed in her face. Looking down at her skimpy attire, she knew she had no choice but to go back to Ty's cabin. Grimly she marched to Ty's door and tried the knob. Locked.

"Ty," she whispered through the crack in the door.

Still no answer.

"Ty!" Forcing his name between her teeth, she glanced uneasily up and down the hallway and tugged on her sash. "Tyyyyyyy!" Damn it. She could feel Roxanne's suspicious eyeball practically laser-beaming a hole through her back from the peephole across the hall.

"Hello." She smiled cheerily at a couple from some Connstarr division or another that Ty had introduced her to earlier that day by the pool.

"Good evening," they answered as they passed, too polite to question why Tyler Newroth's young bride would be loitering in the hallway in her skimpy night wear.

This was ridiculous. "Ty, honey, it's me. Em. The little woman. Wake up and open the damn door," she sang under her breath, and kicked the door viciously with her toe.

Still no answer.

Maybe she could find a house phone somewhere and call him and wake him up, she thought, frantically trying to

figure a way out of this latest turn of insanity. Perhaps
Roxanne would loan hers. Fighting the wave of hysteria that
threatened to send her screaming down the hallway and over
the railing, she balled up her fists and pounded on the door.

"Ty!"

Roxanne's door opened yet again. "Anything wrong?"
she asked, a little too smugly for Emily's taste.

"No, no," Emily hastened to assure her. "Just..."

Ty's door finally opened and he swept Emily into his
arms. "Oh, sweetheart, let's never fight again," he said
dramatically, bending her over backward and thoroughly
kissing her.

"What are you doing?" Emily murmured hazily into his
mouth.

"Saving your adorable little rear end," he rasped, chewing on her lower lip.

"Thanks." She sighed as he carried her back into his
room and shut the door in Roxanne's curious face.

Chapter Nine

"Gin."

"Again?"

"Yep."

Emily tossed her cards onto the pile on the cabin floor, where she and Ty had been playing gin rummy for several hours.

"No fair." She yawned sleepily, then eyed him with mock suspicion. "You must be cheating. How else could you beat me forty-two times in a row?"

"I think you're just letting me win to protect my fragile male ego." Ty grinned and, scooping up the cards, began to shuffle the deck.

"Ha!" Emily yawned again and let her back fall wearily against the floor.

Looking over at her heavily drooping eyelids, Ty smiled in wry amusement. No matter how tired they were, no matter how much they both wanted to curl up in bed and fall asleep, they couldn't. It wasn't safe. No, they had to keep playing, he thought and doggedly dealt another hand.

He was only human, after all. Rolling over onto his stomach, he studied his cards, disgruntled. Here he was, a red-blooded, all-American male, stuck in a room with a delectable, young, red-blooded, all-American woman at three o'clock in the morning, and he couldn't touch her. And beating her at forty-two straight hands of gin rummy did little to improve his suffering state of mind.

What a waste of a perfectly seductive setting. But he'd made her a promise at the beginning of this ridiculous escapade and, being a man of his word, he'd stick to it. Trouble was, back then he'd had no idea how much he would come to care for this little wandering woman of mystery. Or want her. And right now, Tyler Newroth wanted her more than he wanted to draw his next breath of air.

Groaning out loud, he drew a card from the pile.

"That bad, huh?" Emily mumbled, trying to focus on her cards.

"Mmm-hmm." No point in telling her that the image of pinning her down on the floor and doing serious damage to their card pile was the real reason for his groan. "You know, I have an idea that might improve your game."

"Wassat?" she slurred, her head beginning to loll back against the couch.

"Stay awake!" he shouted.

Startled, Emily jolted upright, eyes wide. "Huh?"

Ty chuckled. "Gin," he announced smugly, and laid his cards down on the floor for her to see.

"Already?"

"Yep. Your deal."

"Forget it." Emily tossed her cards at him with a grumpy scowl. "If I'd wanted to play cards all night, I could have stayed in my own room and probably even won some money."

Ty snorted. "I've seen the way you play cards. You'd have ended up in the hole big-time. Besides, I doubt very much that they are still playing cards after all this time."

"Oh, yeah? So what do you think they're up to, Mr. Know-it-all Card Shark?"

"Come on, Emmie. Grow up." Ty smirked and gathered the playing cards into a neat stack. "A man, a woman, a romantic cruise ship. Get real. They're doing the wild thing."

"The wild thing?" She stared at him in disgust.

"Sure. What else would they be doing until 3:00 a.m.?"

"Playing cards," she insisted, a stubborn set to her chin.

"Yeah, right. Who would be stupid enough to sit around playing cards all night, when they could…be doing, uh…"

A smile twinkled in Emily's eyes. "Yes, stupid?"

Slipping the deck easily into its box, he closed the lid and tossed it at her. "Hey, beating the pan—socks off you forty-three times in a row at gin rummy is *not* my favorite way to while away the hours. But I promised you, on day one, that I'd be a gentleman. And," he said smugly, "I'm a man of honor. Not that I wouldn't be interested—if you changed your mind—in … the, uh …"

"The wild thing?" Emily supplied helpfully.

"Yeah." He grinned as she squirmed uncomfortably.

"I can't even imagine poor Uncle Denny and Helga doing … that." Emily's brow wrinkled at the distasteful thought. The logistics boggled her mind.

"Oh, I don't know." Ty shook his head and shrugged. "That Uncle Denny strikes me as a bit of a rascal. And Mom, now there's a party animal if I ever saw one."

"*Yuck!* Stop it." Emily giggled. "I don't want to think about it."

"Why not? Someday, if we're lucky, we'll be their age. And I, for one, hope that we will still have the inclination." As long as he was with Emily, Ty imagined he'd have the inclination till the last gasping breath left his body.

Emily averted her eyes, embarrassed. "Well, I'm going to give them the benefit of the doubt."

"In that case," Ty drawled, taunting her, "why don't you go down there and check on them?"

"No way!"

"Why not? Afraid you might catch them in the middle of a rousing game of strip poker?"

"Cut it out!" she yelled, laughing, and threw the deck of cards at his chest. "I'm going to lose my lunch."

"Not again," he moaned, easily catching the deck before it hit him. They almost didn't hear the light tap at the door over their gleeful laughter.

"Emily? It's me...uh, Mom!" Helga's impressive stage whisper boomed through the door and into the room. "The coast is clear, kiddo. You can come back now."

"Gee." Emily sighed, burying her face in her hands. "Do you suppose she fooled Roxanne?"

Reaching over, Ty smacked her affectionately on her hip. "Don't worry. I'm sure Roxanne is hours into her beauty sleep by now. Lord knows she can use all she can get."

"Then I guess I'd better get going." Emily scrambled to her feet and, grabbing the secret journal that Ty found so intriguing, headed to the door.

"Hey, wait," Ty grunted. Pulling himself up, he limped after her on feet that had fallen asleep. "Oh, ow," he moaned and, clutching her shoulders, leaned heavily against her.

"Mmm. Thanks." He stamped his feet as the feeling began to return. "Now, then," he teased, tilting her face up to his, "I want you to be sure to look for signs when you get back there."

"Signs of what?"

Ty rolled his eyes expressively. "The wild thing. You know—" a grin twitched at the corner of his mouth "—a forgotten necktie, a stray handkerchief, a misplaced cuff link...a pair of boxers hanging from the lamp."

"Argh!" Emily pushed at Ty's strong chest with all her might. "You're terrible."

Ty's grin blossomed as he pulled her close for a kiss that stopped her struggle. "Yeah, and that's why you married me," he whispered, and pushed her into the hall.

* * *

The first rays of dawn broke through the cabin window as Emily pulled her pillow over her head to block out Helga's snoring. Unfortunately the pillow was useless against the renegade thoughts of Ty's handsome face that kept her from peaceful slumber.

For what must have been the millionth time, Emily wished that she could tell Ty the truth—come clean and start over with him on more even footing. Then they would be equals, rather than the host and the parasite, as she now supposed herself to be. But it was too late. The die had been cast.

She would have to live with these frustrating circumstances, and it served her right for lying in the first place. Even though she'd told all these lies with the best of intentions—intentions that included saving humanity—she knew that she'd been wrong. To continue deceiving Ty the way she'd been doing nearly made her sick with wretchedness.

Any future she might have had with him under any other truthful circumstances was lost in a tangled web of lies. A single tear squeezed its way out of the corner of her eye and rolled wetly into her ear.

Maybe, she thought, fiercely brushing at the tears that followed, maybe it wasn't too late for her and Ty to have some kind of relationship—on some level—that was based on trust. She knew that the very least she owed him was the truth after all he'd done for her and the two needy souls she'd foisted on him. Perhaps, when this cruise was over and she'd fulfilled her obligation to him in this matter, she would come clean and see where that got her. Couldn't hurt, she thought, punching her pillow miserably.

Why, oh, why did she have to fall in love for the first time under these circumstances? It was true, she admitted as the morning light became brighter. She was in love. And not with the man she'd stuck her sister with all summer.

Looks like she would have more than one painful confession to look forward to when they returned, she thought mournfully as she finally drifted off into a fitful sleep.

Monday and Tuesday were spent in a blissful haze at sea. Swimming, sunbathing, eating mountains of delectable food, gambling, dancing, moonlight strolls, gentle kisses. Emily couldn't remember when she'd ever been so happy. And, unfortunately, with every minute that passed, she managed to fall more deeply in love with Tyler.

Helga and Denny kept nearly constant company, and Carmen wouldn't hear of leaving her newfound playmates to spend dull afternoons and evenings with the Connstarr management team.

So much of their time was spent as a couple who came and went as they pleased, taking leisurely time to get more intimately acquainted.

In between the normal shipboard activities, Connstarr held meetings, luncheons, get-acquainted parties and social gatherings of all kinds, designed to facilitate team building among its management staff. Emily was not only invited to attend all of these functions, but was encouraged to participate fully right alongside her husband.

For Emily, the only thing that marred her happy experience with the wonderful Connstarr crew was the unsettling feeling that Roxanne was watching her every move. Normally, Emily wouldn't even have minded that, but there was something about the way that troubled woman watched her. Something nearly evil in its intensity. No matter where she and Ty went, Emily could count on Roxanne's dark and brooding presence. Luckily it was rare that she ever needed to leave Ty's side, but on the odd occasion that she did, whenever she returned, she could count on finding Roxanne plastered flamboyantly to her husband's side, laughing a little too loudly, clinging a little too tightly, trying just a little too hard.

Emily was looking forward to arriving at the first port of call, Puerto Vallarta, where they would dock bright and early Wednesday morning. There she was sure they would be able to enjoy a romantic day, far removed from the predatory gaze of her husband's boss.

Unfortunately she'd been mistaken.

Wednesday morning, as Emily took Carmen by the hand to lead her off the ship, Roxanne, managing to beat her way through the line in an effort to catch them, glommed on to Tyler's arm.

"Thank heavens," she huffed, winded by her Herculean effort to reach them before they were out of sight. "I thought I'd lost you." Simpering, she smiled beguilingly up at Ty.

Emily caught his weary glance and shrugged miserably. So much for a cozy family day of shopping and seeing the sights in Puerto Vallarta. Instead they would be subjected to a performance test as Roxanne scrutinized their every move.

"It's lucky you're coming along with us today," Roxanne tossed breezily over her shoulder at Emily. "You can translate for me while I shop."

An angry muscle working in Tyler's jaw brought a smile to her lips.

"*Sí. Con mucho gusto,* I will translate *por me esposo's mega grasa amiga,*" she said pleasantly in a thick Spanish accent, earning a startled giggle from Carmen.

"Thanks." Roxanne darted them a quizzical look, suspecting that she might have just been insulted. "I need to find the perfect little number to wear to the Connstarr Awards Banquet on Friday night. It's only the most important night of the cruise," she informed Ty importantly, "and I want to look spectacular."

Emily blanched.

Turning her back on Emily, Roxanne continued her inane stream of chatter at Tyler. "And, unless you already have your banquet ensemble, we'd probably better get you outfitted, too. Doesn't that sound like delicious fun? The theme for the awards banquet is Mexican," she jabbered, pulling Tyler down the plank and farther away from his family. "Everyone will be wearing something with a local flavor. And since it's simply the biggest event of the entire week, I want you to make an impression, too."

Thankfully for all involved, the excursion finally ended, and after a completely exhausting day of being run around by the energetic Newroth family, Roxanne staggered to her cabin under a load of extravagant purchases and passed out on her bed for the rest of the evening.

When the ship pulled into Mazatlán promptly at 8:00 a.m. Thursday morning, Tyler vowed that he would have a day alone with Emily if it was the last thing he did. Quickly showering, he jumped into the first clean thing he could get his hands on in the suitcase and, checking the peephole for the all clear, pounded down the hallway to Emily's room.

"Psst! Emily! It's me!" he whispered through the door after knocking lightly.

The door opened and he slipped inside. Helga was still communicating loudly with the land of nod as Emily held a finger over her lips to silence him.

"I had the Connstarr sitter take Carmen to the Kiddie Korner this morning," she whispered, pulling her sneakers on and rapidly tying the laces. "All set," she announced, and quietly followed him to the door. "I've got my swimsuit on under my clothes."

Ty's body tensed involuntarily at the thought. "Me, too." Taking her by the hand, he couldn't help being amazed at how well they worked together. It was obvious that Emily craved a day without Roxanne as much as he did, and the thought warmed his blood as they headed up to C-Deck, midship.

How could the slender beauty at his side manage to look so elegant dressed only in a simple pair of light blue shorts and a matching top? Something about her effortless grace and easygoing manner drew him to her like no other woman he'd met before. Something special in her countenance relaxed and stimulated him at the same time. He had the eerie feeling that even though she remained an enigma, there was a familiar quality that he'd known all his life. It was almost as if he had finally stumbled across the other half of himself.

Checking quickly over his shoulder for Roxanne, he tightened his grip on Emily's hand and scurried with her as fast as they dared down the gangway and onto the pier, where they hailed the first available cab.

"Just drive us around Mazatlán for a while," Ty instructed the driver and, leaning back against Emily, sighed with relief. "We did it," he whispered gleefully, pulling her hand to his mouth and kissing the backs of her fingers.

"But not a moment too soon," she said ruefully, pointing back at the ship as they pulled away from the pier.

Ty looked in the direction of her finger and grinned. For there, gripping the ship's rail and radiating a fury that he could feel even at this distance, stood a rather frazzled-looking Roxanne. Her poisonous glare was shaded in chic sunglasses as she scanned the masses for the Newroths. Discovering them just as their cab had pulled out into the early-morning traffic, she watched helplessly and pounded the railing in frustration as her prey escaped her clutches.

"She looked pretty steamed," Emily said, worry tingeing her brow.

"Probably is," he agreed affably. "But that's not our problem, is it, now?"

"No. I guess not." She twisted back around in her seat and looked up at Ty. "I just can't seem to help feeling a little bit sorry for her."

Ty stared down at her in disbelief. "After what she put you through yesterday? You've got to be kidding."

Her features took on an impish quality. "I will admit that she is one tough negotiator when it comes to bargaining for goods and services. I'm sure glad you were there when she got us thrown out of that one marketplace. I thought that several of those shopkeepers were going to string her up alive."

"And I prevented that?" he grumbled good-naturedly. "Why didn't you stop me?"

"Because it would have scared Carmen." A bemused smile tugged at her lips.

"Better luck next time, huh?" he murmured as his eyes darted to her mouth. Mesmerized by the guileless expression he found there, he battled a sudden urge to kiss those captivating lips. Too bad there was no one here to play the part of newlywed husband in front of, he mused, tearing his eyes away from the beauty at his side.

Throwing an affectionate arm around her shoulders, he forced himself to enjoy the scenic beauty outside the cab instead.

"You'd better turn over," Emily suggested, glad for the excuse to study Ty's fabulous torso.

"Hmm?" Ty mumbled sleepily, and opened a lazy eye in her direction.

Reaching over, she pushed a tentative finger into the pink flesh on his chest. "I think you're starting to burn a little bit."

His skin was warm and smooth, and she ached to run her hand over its silky texture. The wind whispered through the palm fronds that stood behind them on the white sandy beach where they'd been lying for the past half hour after an impromptu picnic lunch.

"Um." Rolling over toward her, Ty ran a hand over her hip. "You're feeling a little warm yourself. His eyes locked with hers, and they lay like that for what seemed to Emily like eternity.

The muted roar of the clear, aqua sea as it rolled rhythmically to shore lulled her into the surreal feeling that they were alone in paradise. No Roxanne, no Carmen, no Helga, no responsibilities. Just the two of them, away from all of life's everyday worries and cares.